Zanchier

Book 1

Subjugation

SG Boudreaux

SG Boudreaux

SG BOUDREAUX
Book 1 of the ZANCHIER Series
SUBJUGATION

SG Boudreaux

ISBN: 978-1-7361117-0-3 (Paperback)

ISBN: 978-1-7361117-1-0 (Digital)

SG Boudreaux

Printed in the USA

Sgboodro2@yahoo.com

www.SGBoudreaux.com

To all my loyal fans, who fell in love with
the world of Zanchier that I created for the
Peregrination Series of novels.

SG Boudreaux

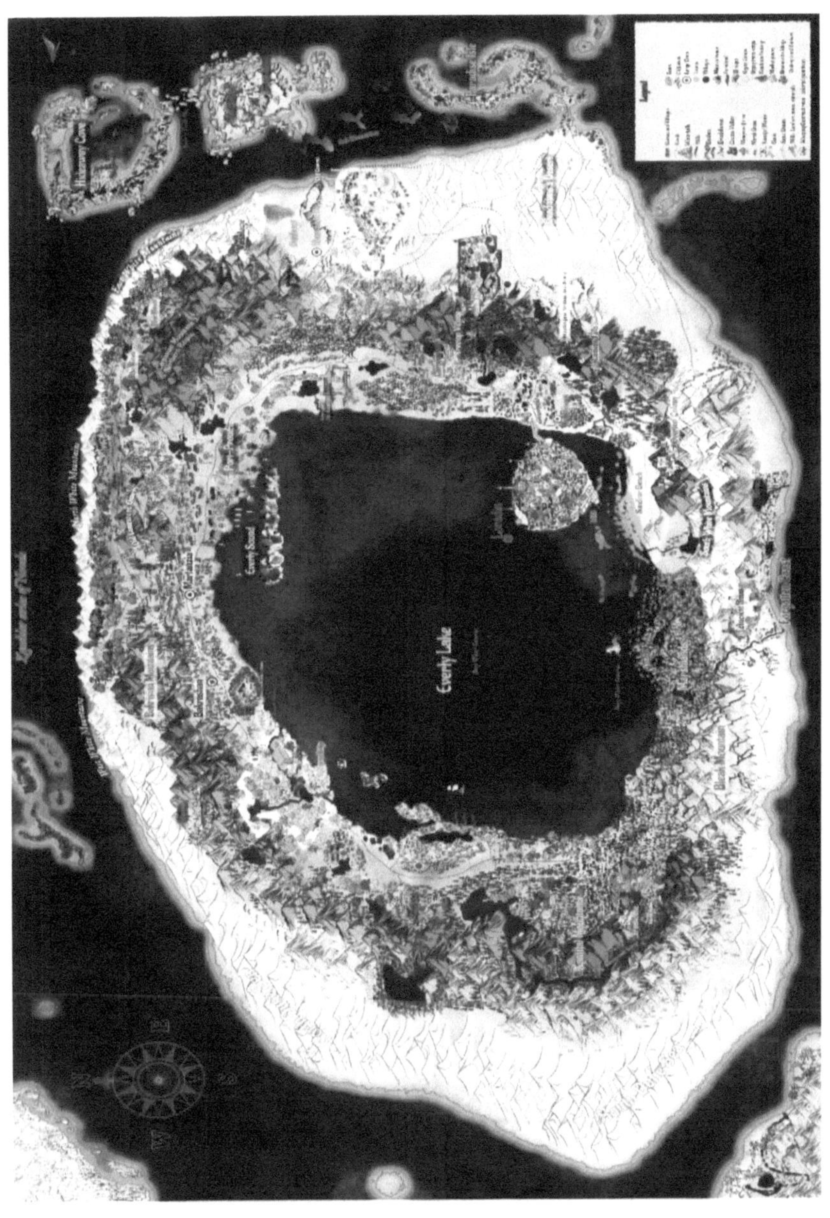

For a better view of the map, sign up for my email list via my website listed in the back of the book on the contact me page. As an email subscriber, you can sign up to get member specials for book-related content for all my books.

Table of Contents

Chapter 1

The Tree

Harper Brinley trudged through the thick, blue, snow that covered the ridge of the Xantifal Mountains. Her three-week journey across Zanchier, from Carpasmere to Bakrashan, had been a rough one. She knew she would be safe and could find somewhere to hide amongst the massive Xantifal Mountain trees. Fortunately, today was a bit warmer than most had been lately. The temperatures had finally climbed up into the low thirty's, making traveling easier.

As she stopped to rest for a minute, the trek up the mountainside making her winded, she stood gazing out over the glistening blue mountains. Fortunately, she had yet to encounter the shifting mountains of Xantifal. And, Storm Valley, which usually was in an almost constant state of bad weather, was quiet this morning.

Harper had heard stories about the valley while she was growing up. The old-timers told them all about a place in the Xantifal Mountains that was in an almost constant state of turbulence with storms occurring several times a week. During cold weather months they occurred less frequently, the rain turning to ice, and the winds blowing in snow drifts.

She breathed deeply of the fresh, cool, clean, mountain air. As the sunrise began to climb higher in the sky, her breath caught in her throat at the magnificence of it all. To see the Xantifal Mountains covered in snow was truly a magnificent experience, especially up on the highest ridge line. The abnormally large trees that graced the mountain's top were covered in the beautiful, glittering, snow. Of course, walking beneath the snow-covered branches could be deadly if one were careless. Most of the tree's branches were so large that a person could walk across them, passing through tree after tree because the branches laced together. If one of those branches decided to let loose its weight of snow, then whoever or whatever was passing below could very well be buried deep within a snowbank until the first signs of Spring began to thaw the frozen landscapes.

Harper took another moment to rest, ever mindful of her surroundings so as not to be taken as a meal by the large Kabihanxus or Pagorinxes which lived around these parts. The Kabihanxu, or firebirds as the locals called them, were large, four-legged, bird-like creatures, whose feathers were of striking colors in golds, blues, purples, reds, yellows, and oranges. These birds looked like fire streaking across the sky as they flew high overhead. They were predators, very territorial, breathed fire, and had an armor like skin beneath their colorful plumage, making them near impossible to kill. They stood about fifteen feet high at the head while on all fours, and their wingspan was twenty feet in length, their body length over half that. Their long, plumed tail feathers spanned out behind them, trailing along the ground as they walked, making them appear as long as their wingspan.

The Pagorinxes, which were very large cat-like creatures, with long sabered teeth on the top row, long, black and white, braided-looking fur, which hung from their body and streaked from the tips of their ears to the back of their haunches. Their coats were so black they almost looked purple at times. Their long sharply curved claws were bluish in color and very deadly. These cats, like the firebirds, were very large in stature, standing almost as tall as the firebirds. These two creatures were amongst the deadliest of all the creatures of Zanchier. There were others, but man at least had a fighting chance against most of those. Most of the creatures here were more of an herbivore nature, so as long as you avoided the two largest, you were pretty much safe.

Harper shivered slightly at the wind as it whistled around her body at the highest point on the ridge. She looked around her to try and find somewhere she might take some refuge away from the bitter cold. She spotted an extremely large tree that appeared to have some open area beneath its gnarled root system. She approached the tree with caution, knowing full well that any number of creatures could have taken up residence beneath the large tree's exposed roots. It was so massive at the base that the light filtering through the trees barely lit the area around the roots, and it certainly did not reach the underneath or center of the tree.

She took out her torchlight and her gun, and slowly scanned the dark underside of the tree's roots, ready to bolt or fight, whichever was required to survive. Other than a few smaller scurrying animals that were frightened by her sudden intrusion into their den, there was nothing that appeared dangerous. She cautiously made her way toward the trees center, noticing that the other side of the tree was firmly rooted inside the mountaintop, its extensive root system intertwined with the soil and rock. With the lack of sunlight streaming into the open area beneath the tree, also came the added coldness of the sunless air around her. She shivered even harder than before, continuing her investigation of the area. She noticed another large hole that seemed to extend up into the bottom of the tree itself. She made her way toward the opening, climbing over the large root system as she went up. She shined her light into the massive hole that, she assumed, sat right in the center of the tree. There appeared to be hardly any dirt at all inside. The large opening was made up of twisted roots that mingled with each other creating walls and a floor of sorts all the way around the interior.

"Well," she sighed to no one but herself, "this might just do quite nicely."

She continued to walk the trees interior carefully, knowing she could stumble upon any manner of creature at any moment. She noticed that the tree seemed to split and branch off on either side of the large center. The large, twisted, roots, and years of compacted wood from the hollowed center, seemed to have formed a set of staircases of sorts on both sides. She chose the left side first, making her way up into a smaller cavity that could be made into a room. It was about an eight-by-eight area. After looking around, she turned and went back down to explore the other set of stairs that went up into the tree on the right side of the center room. The stairs twisted and landed on another small room, a little larger than the other side. But the twisted root staircase seemed to extend even further up. So, she pulled her coat tighter around her body and ascended the staircase further. As she walked up into the interior of what must be some sort of split within the tree, the passage became more narrow, and she was now walking upon the fallen wood of the tree's sides.

She suddenly began to feel the cold air circulating all around her, and she could hear the howling of the wind as if it were blowing through a crack or crevice. As she walked further in, she began to see the faint hints of sunlight streaking through the vanishing darkness. As she walked, she could soon see the fullness of daylight.

A sudden scurrying noise made her jump. She grinned slightly at the sounds of small creatures whose winter nap she had just disturbed. The path soon revealed a large split, which was apparently an area where the trees bark had separated and opened up a long, wide crack in the tree which extended all the way to the inside. She stood there, marveling at the expanse of the split. She assumed the lower half went to the ground, and the wood and dirt in which she walked upon was the rot and fallen wood from where the split had started to begin with. She glanced upward at how far the split went. Flurries of blue snowflakes floated down and landed on the hardened, petrified wood that now made an almost flat floor. It was like being inside a large archway in one of the castles that sat upon the mountainsides in Loradin and Martanzia.

She walked to the edge of the opening and looked down, her head spinning slightly, causing her to lean back quickly.

Goodness! It hadn't felt as though she had walked that high into the tree, she thought. But she could see most of the Xantifal Mountains with nothing to block her view.

"Best not lean out there to far or that will be the end of me."

She stood looking out at the rising sun for a few moments longer before turning to go back down to the tree's interior. After her exposure to the coldness of the crevice with the wind whistling and flowing around her, it was quite warm in the center. She decided to head outside and see if she could round up some wood to make a fire inside to warm herself, and to make a proper breakfast. The large split should allow the smoke from the fire to escape. At least she hoped it would.

After finding some wood to build the fire, she laid down a large, thick, bowl-shaped piece of wood, not daring to build upon the roots of the tree itself. She placed the loose wood inside and lit it. While the fire grew, she prepared the large egg she had found earlier inside a nest, and some of the dried meat she had purchased back at market last week. She cooked the egg and sat and enjoyed the warmth of the fire shrouded by the protection of the tree. This tree appeared to be exactly what she had been looking for. After she warmed up and ate, she would find some wood to try and fashion a sort of door to keep out any wildlife that might decide to make the tree house their home.

While she sat warming her body, her thoughts returned to the day that still constantly haunted her most every waking and sleeping moments; the very reason she was running and in hiding. The day her family was stripped from her. Her children, all taken by the government to make her cooperate with their plans for her to build them a weapon that ran on the Rhenium and Ruthenium that was mined out of the Rhe Mines. She had no idea where her children were, or if they were even still alive. That had been over five years ago. Her husband Wilkins had disappeared one year before that, nearly a year after being forcibly recruited by the government.

Those in charge had decided to place Wilkins into special military operations and had trained him for the position. Before the war, Wilkins had been a farmer. He was born and raised on a farm and had inherited it when his parents had retired to Loradin. Wilkins's father, Aaric Brinley, had struck it rich with a mine deposit of Rhenium that ran beneath their farm's property. He had a naturally formed trench on his property where the line of Rhenium ran just beneath the surface. He had accidentally found the deposit one day while plowing and dynamiting the rock for a new field. He soon after gave the farm to Wilkins who was an only child, and Aaric and his wife Neitha soon moved to Loradin. Wilkins loved the farm life, and despite the "it's a hard life" warnings from his father, chose to stay on. Even though his father gave Wilkins and Harper a substantial earning's check every month from the Rhenium proceeds, Wilkins still chose to work the land, stating that farming was in his blood.

The government tried to claim the mine deposit, but the claim was too far into the middle of their land and they had won the battle. It was only a year after the war had started that they came and recruited Wilkins. He mysteriously disappeared a year later. She figured it had to do with them wanting to get their hands on their property and control one of the largest Rhenium deposits this side of Carpasmere.

When they came for Harper, she refused, stating that she was the only care giver for her children, and she wouldn't leave them. The powers that be stormed into her home one night, took her three children, and put Harper in lock-up, causing her to go into early labor with her fourth child, whom she was told later was still-born.

Harper was then told that if she cooperated they would allow her to be reunited with her children. Her husband, however, was missing in action after a mission he had been on had failed. Harper's father was one of the more powerful men in government and even he had been unable to help her. He couldn't find Wilkins or her children and was unable to secure her freedom. She spent the first year working with other scientists to develop the weapon the government had pushed them for. But before they could work out how to make the Rhenium and Ruthenium power the weapon, some of the resistance fighters had broken into the facility, set the place on fire, and killed some of the other scientists. Harper had barely escaped with her life. She had been in hiding ever since, hoping that they thought her dead. She had dyed her hair from its original red color to black, used digital scanners to change her eye color from green to brown, and used a skin toner to darken her light, freckled, flesh. She barely recognized herself and therefore assumed others wouldn't either. But she took no chances and still hid as far from civilization as she could. She had spent the last two years training with anyone who would teach her to fight and use a weapon. She had grown skilled and had become a force to be reckoned with. She did all of this in the hopes of finding her children one day. She would find them, and she would fight for them, or she would die in the process.

She looked around at her temporary home. Perhaps she would bring them back here to live in peace, away from those who think they can control the lives of others with force and threats. She would find the man who had taken her children that night. She remembered his face vividly and worked hard to remember it so she would never forget him. He would pay for his treachery, as well as those who had employed him and his soldiers.

As she set about the mountainside in search of materials to begin constructing her winter home, she began making plans to find her children and make those responsible for her years of misery pay for it in the worst possible way. She had about three months of hard winter to come up with something. And she would use her time well. She would study the locals that lived at the base of the mountains here, befriend a few who would be useful, gather what she needed, and inquire of those who worked in the government about the possible location of her children. She would give it everything she had to find her family.

Chapter 2

Xantifal Winter

The thick flakes of snow continued to fall, coating the ground and trees in a blanket of cold, frosty blue. The colorful Kabihanxu and the purple blackness of the Pagorinx were quite easy to spot amongst the tall tree canopies, making it easier for Harper to escape becoming an unknowing meal for the beasts.

She worked on making the tree house into a home and just trying to survive the viciously cold, long, winter. She knew she would soon have to take a week or more and head down the mountain in search of supplies and information concerning her family, and anything else that might prove useful. She often would spend the night in one of the town's inns, or she would camp in the woods, far enough away to escape prying eyes, but close enough to not be snatched up by any predators out looking for their nightly meal.

Harper was also cautious about her appearance. She was no raving beauty, but she was an attractive woman. And that in itself would draw too much attention, especially since she was alone. So, when she went into town she covered herself well, and often would find ways to give herself an odor to ward off unwanted advances.

Since the war had started, there was a group of people who fancied themselves above the law. This had always been a problem but had been made worse by the war. The resistance had begun as a group of people battling the evil within the government and its control. It only took a few years for crooked leaders to step in and take that over as well. This new group of outlaws were known as Scaithers. They were ruthless, relentless, and without morals or basic human consideration. To be captured by the Scaithers was worse than being captured by the Zanchieth controlled government.

In Zanchier, each area was known for having a certain group or type of people. The Zanchieths were the wealthy, old-money people who controlled the government, and they considered themselves above taxation. They made up about five percent of the population. Not only did this group put themselves above others, but also their children, and their children's children and so on. As long as their children agreed to a certain type of lifestyle and didn't buck the system, they would enjoy the benefits of a Zanchieth lifestyle.

The next group was the lower-level wealthy. The self-made men and women. These groups were split into two types known as Loradians, who resided in Loradin on the south side of Everly Lake, and the Martans, which resided in the coastal area of Everly Lake's northern boundary, in the city of Martanzia. These two groups were wealthy and controlled the lower levels of government within the city levels. The remainder of the countryside was divided up between these two groups and they ran and controlled the businesses outside the city limits as well. These two groups made up about fifteen percent of Zanchier. They also controlled the upper-level citizens that were classified as the middle class. The Loradians controlled the group known as the Praxers. The Praxers lived within the outlying areas surrounding the larger cities known as Praxtingen. This class existed of about twenty percent of the population, half of that living outside Martanzia in smaller villages. Harper and Wilkins had been classified as Praxers until the wealth of the mine upped their class level. They had wanted no part of the Loradian lifestyle. That decision was probably the very reason their farm had been invaded and taken over.

On the lowest level of citizenship were the hard laborers, and poorer people of Zanchier which made up about sixty percent of the total population. They were known as the Carpasians and the Bakrisians. Most of these people had no other option than to work in the mines. This forced position in the mines was considered payment for the poor living conditions and housing that the Zanchieths bestowed upon them. They brought home very little pay after that deduction. Others ran small, barely profitable booths in the marketplaces, or highly taxed businesses within the villages. Because of this cruel treatment, many people defected and joined with the Scaithers or became wandering gypsies living off the land. The Scaithers considered themselves above reproach and equal to the Zanchieths in every way, actually considering themselves above the Zanchieths and their laws. Hatred for the Zanchieths fueled their every move, which soon spewed over to include anyone and everyone who stood in their way.

Some of the Scaithers did defect from each classification of people, the upper-level citizens being more educated, and therefore preyed upon the needs and the lack of education of the Carpasians and Bakrisians. They again set themselves up as lord and leader and became the worst of all tyrants, again lording over the lower classes. It was a vicious cycle that never seemed to end.

Harper cleared her jumbled mind and tried to stay alert to her surroundings. She could never completely shut her thoughts down. Her mind was always a flurry of memories, ideas, needs; whatever life had thrown at her over the last thirty-five years crept up whenever something triggered a memory.

She ducked her head upon realizing a man had taken undue notice of her.

"Well, now, what do we have here?" came the slurred speech of the already drunken man.

Harper ignored the comment and continued walking, her right hand clasping the hilt of her knife beneath her cloak.

As he walked closer to her and went to reach out for her to spin her around and have a good look, he suddenly stopped and jumped back.

"Ugh…take a bath would ya'? You're smellin' up the whole street!" he yelled after her.

Harper smiled ever so slightly, grateful that the drunken slob at least had some taste and balked at attacking a woman who wreaked. The only problem with the odor was that some people refused to speak to her and give her information. On days like today, she wandered the streets, carefully listening for any information on the war, resistance, Scaithers, or the location of any of the controlling Zanchieths.

Thinking of the Zanchieths brought back memories of her youth. Her parents were Zanchieth. She herself, at one point, had been Zanchieth. That was before she had met Wilkins Brinley. She had fallen for him the first time she had laid eyes on him, and it had been the same for him as well. When they had gotten to know one another, they truly fell in love. Her parents weren't happy that she had chosen outside the Zanchieth group for a life-mate. Her father swore that she would come crawling back to him one day, begging for his help.

She had smiled at him, then looked at Wilkins and said, "Not a chance, Father. I've found my happiness."

Her father had been furious and refused to help her in any way, much to the chagrin of her desperately upset mother. Harper and Wilkins eloped that very hour and had been happily married for ten years when he was taken to serve in the war. The Zanchieths called it recruitment, but it was forced servitude, without chance for return until they deemed it so. Harper had seen many people over the years be recruited and never return. Very few had, and those that did, were never the same again.

She couldn't even remember what had started the fighting. It had something to do with mining rights and who should control which region.

The Loradians and Martanzians fought for years over this very subject and then suddenly there was a civil war within Zanchier.

The Zanchieths had split on whom to support, Loradin or Martanzia. She was never sure which side her father had chosen, but the civil war affected every family on every citizenship level. It pit brother against brother, father against son and daughter, and devastated most mothers beyond recovery. The women of Zanchier were a very broken lot as they watched their families ripped apart in a greed war over mining rights.

The Rhe Mines were rich with Rhenium and Ruthenium. The mineral was in high demand, mostly for its high melting point and ability to be made into some of the hardest metal to be found anywhere. The military powers fought ruthlessly over this, for the armor it created was even Kabihanxu proof. The firebird's hot, steaming, breath could not melt the metal. And even more than that, the metal resisted heating up so the wearer could withstand several attacks from the firebirds. Even to the extent of possibly winning the battle against the deadly creatures. You just had to know where to strike them to penetrate their armor-like skin.

Another benefit of the metals was the weight and pressure it could withstand.

One story she had heard long ago, was about a soldier who had encountered a Pagorinx while on a mission. His troop had run for their lives, leaving him behind. The large cat knocked him to the ground and proceeded to stand upon the man's chest with its large paw. The weight of the cat actually dented the ground beneath him, making an impression in the dirt, but the armor withstood the weight. The cat could not penetrate the metal, lost interest, and walked away.

The man sustained some cuts and scratches from the cat's paws where his body had been exposed, but he was alive to tell the tale. She often wondered if the story were true. It had been circulating since she was but a young girl.

Harper noticed the fishmonger on the corner had some fresh catch today. She glanced at the fish displayed on the table. The pale almost see-through skin of the Bioluminescent fish, called Glowfish, made for an interesting display. They were puffy looking creatures with five long, tentacled arms. Their stings were deadly if you encoun- tered them in the water. Here, they were a delicacy and could even still kill you if you didn't clean them properly. They were pretty tasty too, you just had to make sure you also removed the lumens glands before consuming it or you may start glowing at night yourself. She chose a meatier, tastier fish, and some of the smaller, curved, spiny brines that ran in large schools.

Harper looked at the man whose face contorted with disgust at her odor.

"I'll take two of the large Rockheads and five pounds of the Riverbrine."

"You have rhedon?" he stared at her, expecting her to turn and walk away.

"Yeah. I have rhedon. And I can always take it to your competitor." She stared him down.

"Fine," the man scowled, turning his nose away from her.

"Package it well, I have a long journey and it needs to keep," she said to him.

The fishmonger simply tipped his head to her as he busied himself packaging her order.

Harper watched the town market square trying to gauge which direction to head to next when she spotted an old friend. She handed over payment for the fish and Riverbrine, stuffed them into her pack, and headed toward the tavern where she saw her old friend enter.

When she entered the dark building, her eyes had to adjust before she could tell which direction he went. At the end of the bar, he sat with glass in hand. She walked past him, purposefully bumping into him.

"Hey, watch where you're goin' fella'. And for the sake of all mankind, take a bath," the large man bellowed.

"Sorry for my clumsiness sir," she said, looking him square in the eyes. She noticed his face change to one of recognition before she backed away.

She then went to the furthest corner, away from others so she wouldn't be removed for stinking up the place. She sat there, hiding her face as the tavern owner approached her.

"You gotta' leave. Folks in here can't breathe for the stench you're puttin' out."

"Fine." Harper stood up, glancing at her friend who had just downed his beverage.

They exchanged a slight look before she left the buil-ding. It was only a matter of seconds when he followed her outside and down the shadowed alleyway.

"Harper? Is that you?" Finn Mobley stated in shock.

"Yeah, it's me?" she said, smiling up at the man.

"What on earth happened to you? You smell of dead animal."

"Yes, I know. It was on purpose to ward off unwanted attention. It's working too," she smiled brightly at him.

"Yes. But you're not going to get anywhere else either smelling like that. You know how to fight. Why all the hiding?" he stated curiously.

"I think someone's been tracking me. I thought the hair change, eye scan, and pigmentation would be enough, but I feel someone is still after me."

"I'm pretty sure they all think you're dead."

"Maybe, but I'm not taking any chances. I won't go back. I'm not helping them create the weapon they want. It could wipe out all civilization. They could pick and choose who and what lives with the push of a button. It would be chaos; the power of destruction in every soldier's hands."

"I know. I understand that. I just don't think you need to go this far," he gestured to her stained, smelly robe, tattered clothing, and dirt-streaked face.

"Maybe you're right. I guess I just need to rely on my skills. It's just that I haven't really been able to use them yet and I'm unsure of my abilities."

"Well, you're never gonna' know unless you try. And for sure, no one is gonna' bother you smelling and looking like this. Look, Harper. You look totally different. There isn't a soul who knew you before that would recognize you now."

"You did," she stated.

"Yeah, but I also know what you had done to disguise yourself."

"True," she smirked. "Any news of my kids, or parents or maybe Wilkins?" She knew the last request was one she would likely never get an answer to, but she had to ask.

Finn looked down at the woman he had come to know many years ago through the war. His gaze softened when her voice cracked at the mention of her husband, and the pleading look on her face.

"Not yet. But I go to Martanzia today. I will inquire of my contacts there. Where can I find you if I find out anything?"

"Xantifal Mountain ridge. The highest point," she stated, looking down the alley to make sure no one heard her.

Taken by surprise at her revelation, he yelled, as quietly as possible, "Are you crazy? Harper, it's down-right deadly up there. Not to mention I hear the Scaithers are starting to base some outpost camps around Catamount Gorge. If they catch you, it's over."

"I've already been up there for a month. I found a large tree with an opening at the base. I've made a pretty good place for myself. There is plenty of meat and eggs, and with the snow covering everything, the deadliest creatures are easy to spot. I'm fine. Better than I would be down here."

Finn looked at her questioningly, nervous for his friend. "How in the world am I supposed to find you up there? Not to mention it could take me weeks to make it up the mountainside."

"Not really, just a four-day hike." She said matter-of-factly.

"Maybe for you. You're quite a bit younger than me, remember?" Finn stated irritably.

"Yeah, but there is nothing wrong with the shape you're in, Finn Mobley. Don't try to feed me that old man story. You aren't that much older than me."

Finn grinned down at her, "Maybe not, but I've been ridden pretty hard most of my life and this body sure feels it. Not to mention the weather up there has to be twenty degrees colder than down here in the valley."

"Maybe, but the view is so worth it. It's peaceful there. Which is something I haven't had in a long time," she stated wistfully.

"Fine," Finn conceded, noticing the look of peace that crossed her face. "Maybe I could manage the ride up on my Voyager."

"That two-wheeled contraption?" she stated in disbelief. "I doubt it would climb the mountain. You might even get killed on that thing trying it."

"We'll just have to see. I'm surely not walking it," he grimaced.

"Fine," she said, pulling her hood back over her head, "Just watch out for the Shifts. They get worse and more frequent in the mid-mountain range, just below Catamount Gorge. They don't reach as high up as the ridge line though. Thanks Finn," she said, walking out of the alley-way.

Finn's eyes grew wide at the mention of the Shifts. He swore he'd never go near ground that could suddenly disappear and switch around. Depositing you somewhere else, hundreds of miles away from where you started. And that was if you were lucky. A lot of people fell to their deaths or vanished when the grounds disappeared, never to be seen or heard from again.

Finn shivered at the thought, "I must be out of my mind," he grumbled to himself as he watched Harper disappear around the corner of a building. He shrugged his shoulders and took to leaving, headed for Martanzia and any information leading to the whereabouts of Harper's family.

Chapter 3

A Life Unexpected

Harper returned to her ridge-line tree house high in the Xantifal mountains with her purchased supplies from Treeline Valley. The small mountain-based town was so named for the line of Weeping Giantrush Trees that surrounded it. The huge trees had very thick trunks, and their branches were almost as large as the trees up at the ridge line. Some of the Weeping Giantrush were so large that some people's homes and businesses were actually inside a hollowed-out center, much like Harper's tree house, but none of them could match the size of the tree where she now lived.

The Giantrush's graceful, low-hanging, thinner-tipped, branches of the trees would blow in the spring breezes, gently sweeping the ground in places. The colors of the long leaf tendrils ranged from a bright green in Spring, then turned a purple and sea-blue mixed in with the darker greens of summer. Then when fall would come, the leaves would begin to turn bright blazing red, yellow, orange, and gold before the grayish yellow leaves of winter would wither and die, leaving the sweeping branches barren.

Fall could be a treacherous time of year near the towns, for that was when the Kabihanxu would begin to train their young fledglings to hunt, and they easily blended in with the colorful fall foliage. People tended to pass carefully beneath the trees during this time. And the businesses that were housed within the trees had extra guards on duty around the clock to watch and warn the others of impending danger. Fortunately, not many of the birds would come down to towns like this. They tended to stay high in the mountains where wildlife was abundant, and hunting was easy. But you could never be too careful when it came to possibly becoming a training tool for a young firebird.

Harper had been gone for about two weeks from her tree house and entered the dwelling carefully, never knowing what may have wandered in and taken up residence in her absence. Her door was still closed, but she had no idea of how many possible ways there were to enter the giant tree. Not to mention the large split in the bark and wood of the tree that was opened on the right side. The split went high up into the tree and was located on the opposite side, but still, it was a huge opening. If she stayed on here, she would have to try and figure out a way to seal up the top of it somehow. It would keep out some of the cold drafts that blew in and down the twisted, root staircase.

She ate a meal of fish and bread, hungry after the long journey up the mountain. After which she stored her food supplies in the natural root cellar of the tree, then set about inspecting her home for critters, making a plan for sealing the large split, deciding to make a smaller door for the narrowest part. She then went outside to train for a while, honing her fighting skills. She only had trees and brush in which to fight against but decided to make use of the wood that she laid into during training. Small pieces that she chopped off during training exercises went into the fire pile. When training with her axe she used it on any trees that she wanted to cut down for lumber. In the unpopulated areas of the Xantifal mountains, especially with the Shifts that occurred regularly, there was always plenty of felled, dried timber in which to use in the tree house for furnishings.

Every morning she woke, ate, gathered necessary supplies, and then trained for three hours. She then ate lunch, and wild-crafted what she could from the snow-covered mountainside for medicinal herbs. All the while walking down to the fresh-water springs close to Catamount Gorge to gather water wherever the frozen landscape would allow. Upon returning, she then sat for the next several hours making plans to find her family while fashioning furnishings for the treehouse. During the quiet days and long winter nights, her mind wondered quite often about her past.

When her children were taken from her that fateful evening, no one told her anything other than the threat that if she ever wanted to see them again she would cooperate fully with whatever request was made of her. She had received several beatings early on during her captivity, her anger spurring them. The guards told her once during one of the beatings, that even though they weren't allowed to harm her, no one ever said they couldn't control an unruly prisoner. She had been a *very unruly* prisoner because some of the demands that were made had nothing to do with the weapon they had wanted her to build. Some of the guards had gotten it into their heads that she would be an easy target to have fun with. They soon learned that wasn't the case. But she paid heavily for it. She did notice after one particularly bad beating, when she had been brought to the weapon building room after a long weekend of confinement due to her condition, that the guards who had beaten her were no longer around. Apparently the powers that be, weren't very happy about the condition she was in that day. A half-closed eye due to swelling, bruised hands and knuckles, a busted lip, a few broken ribs, and a limp, made it hard to focus and build their precious weapon. Soon after, she was moved to a more secure area with better living accommodations and her constant guards became women. This alone seemed strange to Harper, but all she could figure was that they wanted her body and mind in top shape for the work that needed doing.

Harper vowed after that last attack that she would never let that happen again. And, if she were suffering all of this, then what could be happening to her children? She had silently built up her strength after lights out. When everyone else was sleeping, she turned her metal framed bed into a training apparatus. Turning it up on its end to do pullups and hanging from it by her feet to strengthen her core muscles. She did anything she could think of to build up her body strength. She had never been week per say, but she had never had a reason before to be as strong as a man, until now.

After the resistance, or better known Scaithers, had broken into the facility, supposedly to kill everyone in sight, she managed to escape. That was the day she had met Finn Mobley. He had been part of the resistance that was supposed to *free* the imprisoned scientists. When he saw his comrades in arms killing everyone, he managed to sneak her out and take her somewhere safe. He left the resistance that day and they became close friends. He trained her himself for a while until she had learned most everything he could teach her. He even introduced her to the Biotech, Kamsten Whitsler, who transformed Harper's appearance so she wouldn't be recognized. Kamsten had been another scientist held prisoner in another facility who had managed to escape as well. She was a mousy little woman around the age of thirty, but highly intelligent, and a bit quirky.

After Harper and Finn parted ways, she sought out anyone who would train her to fight with whatever type weapon available, and to train herself with many different skill sets. She trained with about seven different people over the last three years in between trying to find information about her family.

She had actually sneaked back to her parent's home in Martanzia located about thirty minutes from Port-Proud. But they were not there. She was told that they hadn't been around for the last year and none of the servants knew where they had gone. This of course was after her transformation. She hadn't told the servants who she was, just that she was a friend of Gracelynn Fenore and she wanted to see her. Maybe if she had told them who she was they might have told her differently. Perhaps her parents were in hiding as well. If Harper were a target for the government then her father likely was as well. He was an intelligent man himself and a high-powered business- man with a lot of connections. She wondered often if he had tried to find her, or if he even knew that she had been imprisoned and that his grandchildren had been taken away.

Weeks passed as Harper woke daily with the sunrise, went about her schedule, planned what she would do and say should she ever be reunited with her children, and just plain survived the wild mountains of Xantifal while she waited for any word from Finn.

One morning, she had been sitting outside in the warmer air, carving a new bow, and set of arrows, when she finally heard the distant roar of a motor floating throughout the mountain's canopies, the hum of the engine echoing off everything around her.

"It has to be Finn," she said out loud, jumping to her feet with excitement. It had been weeks since she had seen Finn in Treeline Valley. He was the only person who knew she was here, and the only person she knew who had a contraption that sounded like that. She grabbed her bow and arrows and set out on foot in search of the noise.

She would stop every few minutes or so and just listen to gauge which direction the noise was coming from. At times, the sound would completely fade away for a few minutes. She wondered if she were hearing things for the first ten minutes, but soon the roar would return and echo. The large trees and thick brush made it very hard to decipher from which direction the sounds were traveling. After twenty minutes of walking the ridge line, she finally found the correct direction she needed to go to be able to hopefully run into Finn.

As she walked the semi-open ridge line of the Xantifal mountains, she marveled at the undisturbed beauty all around her. If it weren't for the Firebirds and the Pagorinxes that lived in these mountains, and the shifting of the landscape, the mountains would surely look different than they do now. The government, in their greed to have and control everyone and everything, would have surely destroyed Xantifal and all that made it the magical place it was. The blue snow heavily covered most everything in sight, but in the spring, when the snow melted and the trees and bushes sprang back to life again, the mountain would be bathed in spectacular color. Different shades of purples, blues, golds, and greens would fill the tree canopies, as leaves unfurled, and flowers blossomed and perfumed the air around and below the mountain.

She had never seen this from the top of Xantifal, but all the small villages that dotted the valleys below the mountain's base experienced the same sort of show each year. Harper smiled, imagining seeing such a display of nature from her ridge-top perch and her majestic tree house. Next time she went to one of the villages, she would have to visit a bookstore or historical house to see if she could find a book on trees. She knew quite a few of the trees from survival and nature classes in secondary academy but was unfamiliar with the type that was her tree house. Never had she seen a tree of its like before. There were other smaller ones like it along the ridge line, and a little further down the mountain toward Catamount Gorge, but they didn't go below that.

She shook herself from her momentary stupor and listened once again for the roar of the engine of Finn's Voyager. He had named it that because it took him quickly to wherever he chose to go. Whatever voyage he wished to make could be done quickly with the two-wheeled machine with the handlebar for steering. He had drawn a lot of attention to himself with his invention and had himself been running from the government. Of course, he had been running long before his invention. He liked to tell her that it made his running much easier, faster, and much more fun.

Finn Mobley had once been a highly sought-after assassin. He was well known for never missing or losing a target. He had been employed and trained by the government until they turned on him in an attempt to better control him.

Like Harper, they had taken his family. Finn went on a rampage to recover them from their prisons but was himself captured. To teach him a lesson, those in charge had his wife and children executed before his very eyes. Finn was then thrown into prison for a year before the resistance was formed and some of his old colleagues broke him out.

The very men who once murdered for money became the freedom fighters that the lower-class people of Zanchier hoped would one day free them from the tyranny of the government. The resistance had fought for years making some headway until the resistance itself began to be corrupt.

Harper supposed that Finn had a soft spot for her since her story so closely matched his. She only hoped that her story was different in the fact that her children might still be alive. She hoped that the government thought her dead since the Scaither raid on the camp in which she was imprisoned. The encampment was bombed shortly after Finn had pulled her out of the building. She hoped they assumed that there was nothing left of her to find. Then again, the cell guard she had stabbed and dragged into her cell could have been mistaken for her. She had been a woman of the same build and age as Harper. Perhaps they had fortunately mistaken the guard for herself since she had heard nothing about her escape through the grapevine. Surely the government would have announced her as an escaped convict and offered a reward for her safe return. Especially since they still needed their weapon built. Apparently, there were very few people like herself with the knowledge to build it. It had been years since her escape, and they had been very close to completion of the weapon when the facility was destroyed. Of course, the data to make the weapon was most likely destroyed as well, making them start the whole process over again. But surely they had notes and plans stored somewhere else.

Harper stood at the top of a boulder, overlooking the ridge in all directions. Far off in the distance she could make out the occasional appearance of Finn and his Voyager, climbing the mountainside, headed in her direction. Harper grinned broadly and sat upon the boulder awaiting his soon to be arrival. She couldn't wait to hear if her old friend had found news of her family. She only wished that the news might contain something about Wilkins too. Her heart suddenly skipped a few beats as longing for her husband tore at her very soul.

Chapter 4

The Findings

Finn rode his Voyager up the mountainside at as quick a pace as he could, fighting snowy ground and unfamiliar territory. The further up the mountain he got, the closer he got to the Shifts and the larger trees and animals.

Catamount Gorge could pose a problem crossing if he didn't find a place in which to do so. The gorge, on the highest point, was said to be approximately twenty to thirty feet higher than the water's edge due to Cat Falls where the cliffside was a straight drop down.

Harper hadn't bothered with telling him where he could find such a place and he, crazy enough, didn't bother asking her.

Since there were no roads up into the Xantifal Mountains, Finn had to make his own. He tried seeking out trails, but at the same time he hesitated to travel them. Those trails were made by the Pagorinxes, the large cats that lived around Catamount Gorge and in the central mountain regions. The last thing he wanted to do is have a run in with a Pagorinx. Even the juvenile cats were as large as the massive, twenty-hands high, and eight hands chest-wide Yarequu, which were used to pull carts in the villages.

He stopped the Voyager for a few minutes and turned it off so he could get his bearings on which way he should go. Also, he couldn't hear the Shift's tell-tale rumbling over the roar of the engine of his Voyager.

Finn sat and listened, waiting to feel the shaking ground of the Shifts. He knew from rumor that many people had traveled as far up into the mountains as the gorge and made it back to tell of their adventures. But he knew of no one, except Harper, who had gone beyond the gorge and lived to tell about it.

Years ago, he had heard a rumor about a man who said he was transported to another place by the Shifts. He said he was traveling just below the gorge when he was caught in the Shifts. A few minutes later he was moved from where he was and transported hundreds of miles away to Carpasmere.

Wouldn't that be something? To have to start your journey all over again, hundreds of miles away from where you were just moments before, he thought. That was if you were lucky and survived the changing of the landscapes. The Shifts happened weekly, heard by those who resided around the bottom of the mountain. It used to be that they only occurred a few times a month, but over the years it seemed as though nature itself was in protest, and things occurred more frequently and in a more vicious nature.

Finn listened intently, finding no sounds to alert him to the ground groaning in protest, so he started up the Voyager and continued his journey. He had been traveling up the mountain for a few minutes when a black streak amongst the trees captured his attention.

"Oh, come on! Please tell me that was not a Pagorinx," he grumbled into the air surrounding him. Sure enough, there amongst the large branch-laced trees appeared to be a juvenile Pagorinx, tracking him. It seemed to be very young and just a little awkward in its abilities to navigate the trees expertly. He could probably outrun it if he were confident enough to ride his Voyager at full speed through the forest. However, fear of reaching the gorge in an untimely fashion kept his thumb from full speed throttle. The only problem with this cat being so young was the fact that there was probably a mother close by, willing her young one to be successful in its catch.

Finn scanned the surrounding trees as best he could, keeping his eyes on the trail before him. It seemed as though he could hear the churning rumble of the falls and if he could hear that over the roar of his Voyager then he had to be getting very close. He scanned the trees, not seeing the young cat any longer, but he still wasn't so sure about the mother. His Voyager broke through the edge of the forest tree-line, and sure enough, just about twenty-feet ahead, was the edge of the falls. He turned the handles, and his Voyager slid sideways to a halt, almost sliding him, and it, sideways over the edge. Fortunately, Finn was a strong man and managed to keep control of the vehicle and himself.

"Harper," Finn mumbled to himself, "I could kill you right now." He thought about his almost near-death experience, which could have taken place in several ways. He straightened the Voyager, righted himself upon it, and followed the waterline up the falls to where the water's edge ran level with the ground, trying to find a place to cross. There had to be something, or else Harper would have never been able to get to the ridge line herself. He kept a weathered eye on the forest's tree-line for any movement by animals while riding along the water's edge.

It took about ten minutes for him to find one of Xantifal mountain's famed super trees. The fallen tree was so large and heavy, that when it fell, it embedded about one-third of its circumference into the ground on both sides of the river. Its leaves and upper branches long decayed, while the other end of the tree showed its massive root system, what was left of it anyway, sticking up into the air in all directions. Finn stopped, only long enough to gauge whether or not the log was solid enough to support his and the Voyager's weight.

"Well, here goes nothing. Harper, if I die, I'm coming to haunt you for the rest of your days," he mumbled to himself once more. He maneuvered the Voyager up the branches on the top of the tree and out onto the massive trunk. It was so large it was like crossing a bridge where you couldn't see anything below you. He was careful in crossing, not knowing whether the log had rot somewhere along the way, or he could hit a knot or dip, causing him to lose control of his two-wheeled creation. He rolled his way slowly across with no incidents. When he reached the other side, he took a deep breath and looked back over his shoulder across the wide river. The river's expanse was every bit forty-feet wide, so the fallen tree had to be at least sixty-feet tall and, if he had to guess, about twenty or so feet in diameter.

Finn looked around him noticing that most of the trees up this high seemed to have the same characteristics. He whistled lowly to himself, amazed at the size of almost everything this high up.

Finn throttled the handle, and his Voyager roared to life once again as he cut a trail through the sparse underbrush of the forest floor. It took him approximately an hour to ride up to the ridge line. Fortunately, he hadn't encountered any more of the famed large animals of Xantifal. He hoped the unusual sound of the unfamiliar motor of his Voyager had kept them at bay.

It wasn't long before he recognized the familiar form of Harper Brinley, standing there waving her arms in the air like a lunatic. Finn smiled at her occasional quirkiness when she let her guard down. He came to a stop beside her and turned off the motor.

Finn looked at her broad smile. She lunged at him and threw her arms around his neck to give him a huge hug.

"Whoa, Harper, you about knocked me off this thing," Finn laughed at her excitement.

"Oh, Finn, I'm so glad to see you. It gets kind of lonely up here. The animals aren't much company I'm afraid," Harper smiled and chuckled at him.

"I'm sure it does. I don't get how you're still alive with the size of the animals?"

"Just lucky I guess, or I'm considered small pickings with all the other herbivoracious types of creatures that roam up here. Some are quite large and even more strange looking."

"You know I don't believe in luck Harper," Finn chided her.

"Yeah, yeah, I know. So, what do you want to see first?" Harper stated, quickly changing the subject as usual.

Finn shook his head at her sidestepping the conversation again, "How about some lunch? That was some ride up here and I'm starving," Finn grumbled.

"You're always hungry, Finn." Harper smiled at him with a sideways look.

"I'm a growing man!" he teased.

Harper chuckled at his remark and slung her leg across the back of his Voyager. "That way, sir," she pointed, wrapping her arms around his waist.

"How far and where to?" he questioned over his shoulder.

"You'll see it. Just look for the largest tree on the ridge." Harper grinned as Finn's Voyager took off across the mountain top.

Finn steered the vehicle across the wide ridge, dodging the new growth of small trees and brush that was scattered across the ridge of the Xantifal Mountains. "Any dangerous holes, or drop offs I need to be concerned with?" Finn yelled over his shoulder.

"Nope. It's pretty clear from here. It isn't too much further ahead," Harper yelled back.

Finn rounded a stand of large trees, pulling the Voyager to a sudden stop.

"Whew…," Finn whistled at the sight of the massive tree that sat in front of him. They were still a bit away and it was already overwhelming. It wasn't the only large tree, but the extremely large diameter of the trunk and thickness of the swooping and interlocking branches was hard to believe. The large split that ran up the side of the tree made him curious as to what would have caused it, but it just added more character to the tree, and apparently didn't cause any harm to it.

"Impressive, isn't it?" Harper grinned at his reaction.

"That's an understatement. I've never seen anything like it," he said, turning the handle and making the engine roar to life. They continued forward until they reached the tree, with Harper instructing Finn where to drive beneath the large, exposed, root-system. He parked near the entrance and the wooden door that Harper had fashioned to fill the hole into her make-shift home.

Finn stepped through the door into the open space of the interior of the tree as Harper showed him the layout and gave him a tour of the place. Afterward, they sat down to lunch, and to discuss what Finn had discovered in his hunt for Harper's family.

"Harper, you've done pretty well for yourself up here. It's hard to believe that you were once just a farm girl."

"Hey, farm girls have skills," she said, feigning wounded feelings. "Farming is a lot of hard work, family, animals, long hours, unladylike strength, and problem-solving skills."

"Yeah, I know. But to live here alone, that's no small task. Especially with the large beasts that roam around. I truly don't know how you're still alive. But I'm glad you are," he finished with a toothy smile.

"Thanks," she smiled back. "It is lonely, but peaceful at the same time. I prefer the latter, seeing as how the only company I've had lately has been unsavory."

"Hey!" Finn protested.

"Except for you of course," she smiled apologetically, knowing he was chiding her. "I've just been on the run for so long, Finn, that it has been really nice to not have to."

"I get that," he said with understanding.

"Okay, enough beating around the bush," Harper said, looking her friend in the eyes. "Did you find out anything about my children?"

Finn adjusted in his seat nervously and cleared his throat. "Yeah. I found them."

Harper couldn't contain her excitement, "Where? Where are they, Finn?"

"At your parent's place."

"My house? But the doorman said they weren't there, and no one knew where they had gone," Harper replied, confused.

"They have a new place, on the outskirts of Port-Proud in Everly-Sound."

"I don't remember my parent's ever having a place in Everly-Sound before," Harper stated confused. "What on earth would they be doing in Everly?"

"Maybe they were just running too, Harper."

"Maybe. But, if you found them then surely whoever was hunting us would be able to find them in Everly? It isn't exactly a low-key kind of place. Of course, my parents weren't ever ones for living the low-key lifestyle either."

Harper's demeanor changed when she realized her children were safe in the care of their grandparents.

"Oh Finn! Thank you so much for locating my kids," she said smiling as she threw her arms around the man's neck in appreciation.

"All right, all right," Finn said, patting her on the back and pulling away. He was never one for any type of affection, and Harper definitely had put him out of his comfort zone hugging him all the time.

Finn sat her at arms-length as she grinned at his discomfort. "So, what now, Harper? What's the plan?"

"I don't know exactly. I've been dreaming of this day for so long, and I have gone over it time and time again in my mind, wondering what I would do. I guess I just never expected them to be taken care of. I think it's time I paid my parent's a visit."

"You don't exactly look the same."

"Exactly. So, it shouldn't be too hard to get in to see them, should it?" she grinned happily, as Finn wondered just what she was thinking, almost seeing the wheels of her mind beginning to form a plan.

"What exactly do you have in mind? You still need to be careful you know? Especially around people who knew you well. You may not look the same, but your mannerisms are. And they may very well get you into trouble. The people who took you studied you for years first. Trust me, they know more about you than your parents probably do. They may think you're dead, but if you draw the attention of the wrong person, then they might could catch you again," Finn stated, worried that his friend would soon find herself in trouble once more, and he probably wouldn't be able to get her out of it this time around.

"Stop being such a worry-wort, Finn Mobley. There is no way I'm going to miss the opportunity to see my kids. I may not have the power to have them with me right now, but they need to know that I am alive and that I did not voluntarily leave them. I will figure out a way for all of us to be together again, but for right now, I'll settle for just seeing them again."

Chapter 5

The Brinley Children

Fifteen-year-old Bain Brinley shuffled through the hallways of the Port-Proud Academy for the Technically Advanced and Gifted youth of Zanchier. The academy gave scholarships to about 100 students from the Carpasian, Bakrisian, and Praxer regions of Zanchier each year. The Martans and Everly-Seaport citizens could afford the tuition. The Zanchieths had their own training academy. They were too good to even attend academy with the rest of Zanchier's population.

Since Bain's father had disappeared over six years ago, and his mother was taken away from them almost a year later, he had been hyper focused on his future. He and his three siblings had not seen or heard from his mother in over five years. He knew for sure she had been alive when they had taken her because his baby sister Adda had been brought to them seven months after his mother had disappeared. They weren't told anything else. He hoped and prayed often that *she was* still alive, but they had not heard from or seen her in so long that he was beginning to give up hope.

His younger-brother Seadon vaguely remembered their mother, and their younger sister Wynne was much too young to really remember her at all. Their baby sister Adda never got a chance to know mother, being taken directly from her at birth. He wondered if mother ever even had a chance to see Adda herself? Fortunately, their grandparents had been more than willing to take them in. Their grandmother was very upset about Harper's disappearance, but very pleased to have her grandchildren living with her, since they were the only things she now had left of her one and only child. She took the role of mother very seriously, too seriously sometimes he felt, but at least the government had not split them all apart. Bain remembered the first six months after they had been brought to their grandparent's house. He remembered his grandmother and grandfather arguing over Grandfather's influence in the state, and how Grandmother couldn't understand why he couldn't figure out what happened to Harper, or who had taken her, or what they were doing to her. His grandfather had assured his grandmother that he was doing everything humanly possible to find Harper or any information leading to her whereabouts. Grandfather had assured grandmother that she was most likely fine, and as long as she did what the government wanted they would release her soon to return to her family. Bain knew that his mother was some sort of technical whiz, most likely where he got his intelligence from. He also knew that while she had been taken by the government, he didn't know why. He just knew it had to do with her intellect and scientific abilities and knowledge. His mother had told him that his father had been taken because the government wanted their land and the mining rights that ran deep beneath the soil of their farm. She had confided in Bain but asked him to tell his younger siblings very little about the situation. She hadn't wanted to frighten them, but she knew Bain was old enough and smart enough to be able to handle the truth.

Suddenly, someone ran into Bain knocking his books from his hands. He watched as his books and papers flew across the hallway floor.

"Watch it, brainless," came the snide remark. Bain knew who it was without even having to look up. His least favorite person in all of his academy experience, one Riglan Mortruff and his two misfit companions. They had been at odds since primary academy. Riglan was a very bad sort and treated most everyone the same way he did Bain, but for some reason, he disliked Bain the most. Bain began gathering his books and papers, stuffing them underneath his arm while he questioned Riglan.

"What do you want now, Riglan? Have you already reached your quota of torturing the younger masses today and decided to move on to the rest of us?" Bain asked with exasperation and raised eyebrows.

"Nah, just thought I'd treat you to my special kind of attention today, Bain," Riglan had the most weasel-like smile that Bain had ever seen for someone who was only sixteen.

"Gee, thanks for the consideration, Riglan, but I don't have time to play with you today," Bain said, side-stepping around the boy who was equally matched to himself in height and size.

"Aw... now that's too bad, Brainless. What's got you all in a tizzy today? Off on another mission to find dear ole departed mommy and daddy?" Riglan teased.

Bain almost stopped in his tracks, references to his parents making him edgy especially coming from the likes of Riglan. But, if he let him get to him, he would never be able to get to the historical-house and finish the search that he had started a little over a year ago, when he had heard his grandfather say something about the possible location of his mother. Since then, he started doing research on the facilities and the government as secretly as possible. Only problem was, Riglan had seen some of his research and notes one day in one of his notebooks and had pieced together what he was doing. Now Bain had to be extra careful because Riglan would do anything to get him into trouble, just to give him grief.

Bain ignored the remark and continued walking as he heard Riglan and his cronies snickering behind him as he walked away. None of the kids at academy really liked Riglan, everyone tried to ignore him as much as possible but sometimes it was just too difficult. Bain wasn't even sure how Riglan had been accepted to this institution. He probably got in by the influence of his grandparents. Riglan's father was high up in the government somewhere. Bain knew this by listening in on his grandfather's business meetings or overhearing his phone conversations. The name Vonder

Mortruff came up often, and usually with a tone of despair in his grandfather's voice.

Bain's thoughts returned to how Riglan got into Port-Proud tech. He wasn't exactly a real intelligent fellow. Not to mention that he was already sixteen and still in academy, and this particular one was for advanced students and the very gifted technologically minded, and Riglan was in no way advanced or technical from what Bain had witnessed over the years. He wasn't stupid though, Riglan was really smart, just in a sinister, scheming type of way. He had a propensity for evil doings and seemed to excel at it, heartily enjoying himself in the process.

Bain ducked into the historical-house, found the most remote, unoccupied uplink he could, plugged in his scrambler-anti-tracking device that he had created in programming class so that he couldn't be tracked by anyone, especially the government, and set about his search once again.

"Now, let's see…," Bain mumble to himself as he scanned the room with his eyes, making sure no one was within earshot, or paying undue attention to him. It only took him a few minutes to get into the government's secret databases. He had been searching them for the last few weeks trying to find any information that may link to his mother or father. He didn't know a whole lot of information about either of his parents other than the standard stuff. He was so young when they disappeared he really hadn't paid attention to a lot of things that were taking place. Now he wished he had. He wished he'd asked more questions and paid more attention to the little things, but none of them ever thought something like this would happen. There was no point in beating himself up about what he couldn't change, but it made him very focused on what he could.

He ran a cell block search of all the locations where prisoners were held that he knew of. He had run across a few names of places while searching that he had never heard of before. Could they be secret holding bases or some other type of secret government facilities? But it was going to take him several more weeks just to run through the normal prison system files for criminals. Of course, now that he thought about it, his mother wasn't the standard prisoner. She had broken no laws and she'd been taken without reason. Perhaps she wasn't in the prison databases after all. After this thought, he decided to change directions and search one of the other unknown names he had found within the databases.

"Vassalage, that's an interesting name," he mumbled, staring at the screen and the four other listings, none of which gave any information about what kind of organization they were.

"Hey, Bain. Whatcha' doin'?" Bain quickly hit a button shutting down the program, turning to see who had sneaked up on him. Bain let out a sigh of relief when he realized it was just his friend Kreelie .

"Dude, you scared the life out of me. Stop sneaking up on me when I'm concentrating on doing computer work. You know I can't be caught with what I've been doing," Bain said, slightly aggravated.

"Then why do you do this stuff here at academy? It's not like you don't have the best uplink system at home. I don't know why you just don't do it there."

"I *do* work at home. But I have some down time here and every second counts. Besides, at home I have to contend with my siblings always wanting to know what I'm doing or wanting to play or hang out. When I'm at academy I can look without interference. Usually," Bain finished with a look of reprimand at his lifelong friend Kreelie Rintel.

"Soorryy!" Kreelie said, raising his hands in the air in apology.

Bain grinned at his friend and patted him on the shoulder, "Eh, it's alright. I probably shouldn't be doing it here anyway. If I get caught, it's going to be big time punishment, and probably from more than just the academy. Besides, my grandfather could probably get into a lot of trouble too."

"Exactly, so what you're really saying is I just saved your life?" Kreelie smiled brightly at Bain.

Bain looked at his friend, cracked a lopsided grin, and slapped him in the chest with the back side of his hand.

"Sure, Kreelie. If that's what you wanna believe. How about we go see if the cafeteria has anything good to eat for lunch today?"

"Great idea, Brainless, I'm starvin'," Kreelie teased.

"Hey, I get enough of that from Riglan," Bain warned in a friendly manner.

"Yeah, But I say it with caring and friendship." Kreelie made a grand showing of emotion and drama.

"You really should have taken that acting class. I think you missed your true calling," Bain stated.

The two boys chuckled at their antics as they walked to the lunchroom in search of something to fill their growling stomachs.

Seadon Brinley, age thirteen, and second born son to Wilkins and Harper Brinley, attended Port-Proud Primary Academy. Since first attending at the age of eight years old, he was placed into the Future Airmen of Zanchier Training Program, or FAZ for short. Seadon had demonstrated at an early age the propensity toward flight with his many models, and by trying out a pair of homemade wings and leaping from the second story balcony of the boat house into Everly Lake. This attempted flight gave his grandparents quite a fright and convinced them to place him into the FAZ class as soon as he came of age to be accepted. Grandfather had decided that if he was that determined to fly then he best learn how to do so properly. And it was something he excelled at. He hoped to one day be the top airman at Martans Air Academy and be the first to fly across Zanchier in the new airships that were being built.

The government had been mining Rhenium and Ruthenium from the Rhe Mines trying to find the exact formula that would allow the airships to be able to hold up against Kabihanxu attacks. So far, all their attempts had failed, but their instructor had informed them just last week that a new scientific formula had recently been developed that they believed would withstand the firebird's hot molten breath, and razor-sharp talons. The thought of sky flight thrilled him, and the chance to outwit and outrun a firebird thrilled him even more so. As he excitedly hurried toward FAZ classes, he grinned broadly at his sister Wynne who was passing him in the halls.

"Hey, Wynne," Seadon beamed.

"Hey, Seadon," Wynne smiled back. She and her older brother by two years had a close relationship. He was terribly protective of her and they got along great. Much better than she and Bain did. Oh, Bain was a good brother too, but lately he was preoccupied by whatever new technical toy he had invented. He was always on his computer, and never had time for any of them anymore. Wynne just figured it was due to his teenage status and dealing with that horrid bully Riglan Mortruff. Thank goodness Riglan didn't have any siblings. It spared the younger generations from more Mortruff torturers.

Wynne wasn't like her brothers. She wasn't exceptionally smart like Bain, or extremely brave and daring like Seadon. Wynne was just plain, ordinary, Wynne Brinley. She had no distinguishable traits or talents as of yet. Of course, she was just eleven years old. Perhaps she would be a late bloomer. She loved animals and nature, but that wasn't a talent. Most children knew what they were to be by the age of eight. If Wynne couldn't find a talent within the next two years, then her future would be an uncertain one. They were expected to enter the work force by the age of sixteen, unless they went on to government training facilities for further instruction, but that only happened to the technical wizards and the gifted citizens. Usually by age eight, they were sorted into their called fields for specialized training. A few, like her, were just taught general skills until such time as their talents appeared. Wynne stressed over her lack of talent, in which her grandmother assured her that she would certainly one day find her place. Even if it were just to marry well and be a wife and mother. But still, even the wives and mothers had talents and careers. Wynne had heard tales of what befell those like her who had never found their talents. They were carted off to the mines or the harvest fields. Theirs was the life of hardship under brutal taskmasters. Like much of the lives of the Bakrisians and the Carpasians. That wasn't a life she wanted or would accept. She would lie if she had to. She was a hard worker and quite an actress if need be. She would fake it if she needed to avoid the mines or harvest fields. Wynne turned the corner of the hallway and walked into her general studies classroom, forming a plan in her head to decide what kind of talent she might want to find in herself as soon as she could muster how to learn something well and quickly.

Chapter 6

To Claim My Own

Harper and Finn spent the next week finishing off her new bow and arrows, gathering supplies for the week-long journey to Everly-Sound, and forming plans A, B, and C in the attempt to see Harper's kids.

First she had to figure out how she was going to get inside the house. Then she needed to decide if she was going to allow her mother and father to know she was there. She wanted as few people to know who she was as possible.

Harper thought about her children.

"Finn, do you think my kids will even remember me? I mean, I know they won't recognize me, so I may need to change my appearance back before doing this."

"That's not a good idea, Harper. You would have an easier chance going like this. Your kids may not recognize you, but like you said, it's been five years. Bain and Seadon are likely the only ones who were old enough to really remember you anyway. Wynne was only five years old."

"I know," Harper stopped what she was doing and turned to look at him. "Do you think I'm doing the right thing, Finn?"

"What do you mean, Harper?" he asked quizzically.

"They haven't seen me in *five years*. I know they are being taken care of with Mother and Father. Perhaps they are better off without my interference?"

"Look, Harper, whatever you decide to do is up to you. But if I had the chance to see my family again, and hold my wife and kids, nothing would stop me. Your kids have a right to know their mother. And I'm certain Bain and Seadon would make things all right with your youngest girl."

"I know, it's just that they've been through so much already with the disappearance of Wilkins six years ago, and then me for the last five years."

"Exactly. They deserve to have their mother with them."

"I wonder what my Mother and Father are going to say? Father never really liked my decision to marry Wilkins. He wasn't a Zanchieth, and Father had high hopes for his *brilliant-minded* daughter," she said sarcastically. "He tried *so hard* for the first year after I met Wilkins to discourage our relationship, but he failed. He even basically disowned me for years until after Bain was born. Mother was so angry at him that she couldn't see her grandchild, that he eventually conceded to her and they began to come for visits. Father only came because Mother threatened him that if he didn't come she would leave him. He finally began to warm up to Bain, and eventually even Wilkins, especially since he found out that our little farm sat on one of the largest deposits of Rhenium and Ruthenium that had ever been found."

"Humph," Finn mumbled, "Money always turns the heads of the greedy. I should know, I used to be one of them."

"Yes, but now you are my hero, rescuer, confidant, and best friend. Only friend actually," she laughed. "You are the only person in the entire world that I can depend on, Finn."

"Only one you can see that is."

"Now let's not start all that Creator talk. You know I don't believe in all that higher power stuff. Besides, if that were the case, and a higher power existed, then why would He, or She, or it, allow all the things that have happened to me and everyone else? No. If there is such a being, I don't think I want anything to do with them. I will make it just fine on my own, like I have for the last five years."

"On your own huh?" Finn stated, looking at her.

"You know what I mean. Of course, you have done a lot for me Finn, and I am forever and eternally grateful. But I have had to survive on my own for most of that time."

"Yeah, I know, Harper. But if you'd just listen, you'd realize you wouldn't have to. The Creator can help in ways you can't possibly imagine." He stopped talking, throwing his hands up in surrender at the look she gave him.

"Okay, I'm done. No more Creator talk."

"Great. Now let's get to the task at hand and make some plans to see those kids and parents of mine. Surely Mother and Father will also be happy to see me too."

"Harper, I can't imagine anyone not being happy to see you," Finn assured her.

She smiled at him with a grateful heart. Finn was a good friend and had been since the day he pulled her out of that encampment all those years ago. She was lucky to have him in her life.

"All right, so, what's plan A?"

"Well, if I enter into the house as a servant or an employee for one of their many yearly dinners then that would be an easy entry inside."

"What if they no longer have those dinners? Things have changed a lot in Zanchier Harper. Not just at the lowest levels but in the higher ranks as well. Your parents are no exception."

"I know that. But, if they have a reason at all to have a party, they will. There must be a list of planned parties on the Zanchieth government webpage of all the events that are scheduled for the new year. The Social Events page on the up-line server should be able to tell us."

"And where do you expect to find an uplink to be able to look for this information?"

"Surely one of the villages in the valleys will have one, or we can look at the historical-house when we get into Port-Proud."

"Those public uplinks are all monitored by the government. It might raise a red flag?"

"I don't think so. There are lots of people who check the Social Page around the beginning of the new year. No one wants to miss an event if they can make it. People trying to reach that higher status you know, and most willing to do so by any means necessary."

"All right, what if that plan fails? What next?"

"Then we sneak in during the dark of night."

"That's a sure-fire way to get caught, Harper. Surely your parents have alarm systems on their home entryways."

"Yes, but they likely still have the same passwords they used while I was growing up. I bet I can deactivate the alarms easily."

"Okay. That's A and B. What's plan C?" he sighed.

"Plan C? Find out if I can see them at their learning academies. They aren't protected areas except for the scanners located at the doors entering and exiting the buildings. And with my new appearance, I shouldn't be recognized."

"That might work, but what if that plan fails as well?"

"If all else fails, we simply run. If the first three don't work, then we run and live to plan another day."

"Okay. Let's nail down all the details. Where to meet and how to reach each other in case you get caught."

"Well, we can't exactly plan that until we see the area and get a feel for the layout of Everly-Sound and Port-Proud."

"True. All right then. Let's gather our materials and get packed and ready to go."

"This may sound strange, but I'm really going to miss my mountain top treehouse. I've grown quite fond of it up here."

"I understand what you mean. It is peaceful, except for the eerie shrieks and roars of the carnivorous animals at dawn and dusk."

Harper grinned at his sarcastic reply and continued with a serious one. "Perhaps I could bring my kids back here to live."

"Do you really want to give your kids a life of isolation, Harper?"

"No. But I also don't want them used and mistreated by the very people who are supposed to protect them as citizens of Zanchier. Those in charge of the government have obviously abused their powers. I don't believe there is anyone good left, and if so, they have probably been dealt with as well."

"You're probably right, but I know of a few powerful people who are trying to restore Zanchier to its former glory of prosperity and equality for all of its citizens. They've even been playing with the idea of forming an actual resistance again. Just hearsay mind you, but it was strongly talked of several months back. Some of my contacts higher up said they were considering forming an alliance with other like-minded people in the surrounding cities as a matter of urgency. When we get to Port-Proud, I'll try to get in touch with my contacts and see where this has all gotten to."

"Well, hopefully this resistance will be better than the last one and not turn on the people like the Scaither group."

"I believe that group was started under the farce of good to gain power and guns by those higher ups that wanted to takeover ruling offices."

"We shall see, Finn. Let's get packing."

Harper and Finn made short work of gathering their supplies, especially since Harper owned very little to begin with. It was still early morning, just a few hours after sunrise when they straddled Finn's Voyager, ready to set out across the mountain and leave Harper's treehouse far behind.

She glanced over her shoulder for one last look at the snow-dusted tree as the sun's rays began to heat up the morning and melt the glistened blue snow of Zanchier. She smiled wistfully and turned her attention back to her future, as parts of her past began to become only memories.

"All right, Finn, I'm ready to go claim what's mine."

Finn nodded and started his Voyager. Harper held tightly to Finn's waist as he rode his Voyager across the ridge line of the Xantifal Mountains in the direction of Everly Lake. The trip would likely take them a full week to make. It had taken Finn that long to find Harper once he garnered the information he was looking for, but then he had an uncertain destination. The trip back down the mountain may be a bit quicker seeing as how they knew exactly where they were headed.

"Finn," Harper yelled over the engine's roar, "I have to admit, your contraption is quite fun to ride!" Finn glanced back over his shoulder at the smile on Harper's face and he smiled and chuckled at her expression of joy.

"Well, you just hold tight. This ride will most likely be quite bumpy," he yelled back as she shook her head yes and grasped him tighter.

There weren't any pathways to follow but Finn just tried to pick the path of least resistance. He remembered how far down the gorge was and wondered if it snaked around both sides of the mountain. They would head north toward Bakrashan and Martanzia. South was the barren lands that took them toward southern Praxtingen. He had come up the mountain from Treeline Valley, figuring it to be the closest straight line to Harper and the Ridge. Directly east lay northern Praxtingen and west was the long side of the mountain and nothing but wasteland and desert.

Finn's Voyager was slow going through the heavily wooded area and thick underbrush of the snow-covered mountainside. They had to stop several times to get their bearings, as everything was beginning to look the same in the woods.

Harper and Finn listened intently to the sounds of the forest that surrounded them. They could hear the distant rumble of something. Was it the thunder in the valley, or could it possibly be the Shifts beginning? Harper and Finn nervously looked at each other.

"Finn, I think maybe we ought to get out of here!"

"I believe you're right, Harper!" Finn stated, growing a bit nervous as to the growing rumbling sound and the now obvious shaking of the ground beneath them.

Just at that moment they both heard the piercing cry of a Firebird somewhere above them in the sky. They were pretty sure that it wasn't searching for them since they were basically covered by the canopy of the trees. But that made them wonder what it could be searching for? It wasn't long before they heard the growl high above them in the canopy of the trees. They both glanced at each other nervously, fearful as to what was about to take place. Neither of them had realized they were being hunted by a Pagorinx, but apparently it had been following them in the tops of the trees. Finn glanced at Harper with a warning to wrap her arms around him tightly. Finn started the Voyager and took off as quickly as he could manage across the rough terrain. They could hear the brush thrashing and the upper treetops smashing together as large deposits of snow fell to the ground behind and beside them. Harper kept her eyes to the tree canopies, trying to stay focused on the streak of black, teal, and white fur moving quickly throughout the branches, keeping almost perfect time alongside the Voyager, tracking its prey, ready to pounce at any moment. Harper urged Finn to move quicker, feeling the cat was ready to attack at any second. The ground underneath them began to shake and rumble as the trees and bushes alongside them began to sway and fall as well. Some of the trees alongside them fell into nothing as the ground beneath them began to disappear.

"Finn!" Harper screamed over the noise of the Shifts, the now screaming cat in pursuit, and the roar of the engine, "I'm not sure what would be worse, the Pagorinx attack or the Shifts!"

"Well Harper," Finn yelled back, "we're about to find out!"

Just as the cat leaped from the trees, about to land in front of them, it was snatched out of the air by the largest Kabihanxu either of them had ever seen. Luckily for them the Pagorinx was now struggling to free itself from the large claws of the Firebird as the epic air battle took place before their very eyes. The Firebird struggled to hold onto its prey. The Pagorinx was nearly as large as the bird itself. As Harper and Finn watched the struggle, they were caught up in the middle of the Shifts and transported to the other side of the mountain in a matter of minutes. The landscape around them changed drastically and they were now on much flatter land. It took them a few minutes to figure out where they were, realizing that they had been displaced several hundred miles to the south near the end of the Xantifal Mountains and the Bakrashan territory.

Harper sighed in frustration, "No way. I can't believe we are another couple of days further away from where we were headed."

"At least we didn't die during the Shifts or become breakfast for a family of Pagorinxes." He sighed heavily, grateful to still be alive and thanking the Creator for their salvation.

Harper grinned at his exhortation, "You know something, Finn," she said, "I may just be starting to believe in this Creator theory of yours. He sure does seem to deliver you from an awful lot of situations."

"Harper," Finn answered her, "there's a lot worse things you could do than to believe in the Creator."

With that being said, they both grinned and sighed deeply, happy to be alive. They set out on the Voyager once more, now in much flatter territory. They knew they were somewhere near the furthest end of Bakrashan, but where exactly it was they were deposited was still somewhat of a mystery.

They drove for nearly an hour before recognizing they were now in Treeline Valley. From there they were able to figure out how long before they would reach Port-Proud in Martanzia.

Chapter 7

Well Laid Plans

Harper and Finn pulled into the large bustling city of Port-Proud three days later. Harper began to get lost in memories as Finn navigated the Voyager through the city streets. Everly Lake was just on the other side of the city on the outskirts of town. It was a massive body of water that sat directly in the center of Zanchier. It was so large that some of the old-timers say that the entirety of the lake had yet to be explored to its fullest. It was surrounded by the mountains of Xantifal and Carpasmere, with a small pass on the south side. All the major waterfalls of the Xantifal Mountains and the Carpasian Mountains flowed into the lake. There was one particular waterfall known as Luminesce Falls where bio-luminescent creatures and algae thrived. The falls glowed brightly on nights where the moon was dark. Some of these creatures found their way into Everly Lake. On darker nights you could see schools of glowing fish swimming below, creating magical, mesmerizing, rhythmical movement just below the water's surface. It was beautiful to watch, but swimming with some of these fish was a deadly thing to attempt. Some were highly poisonous. One sting from a tentacle and you were a dead man, a slow painful death as the poison seeped into every cell, swelling every piece of tissue in your body until the inevitable end. At that point people begged for death. Everly Lake was a place of immense beauty and color, but caution had to be used when living near the water or partaking in water activities.

Everly-Sound was a stretch of land that extended into the lake for about five miles. It was approximately a half mile wide at its widest portion and at its most narrow, only large enough for the two-way road to pass through with only about ten foot of shoulder on each side. You had to cross Everly

Bridge to reach the island. Even though technically, the island was a peninsula, the part of the land that connected the island to the shore was so narrow that you couldn't even see it as it sat just below the surface of the water. Everly Bridge was built by the government at the request of the Martans and Zanchieths as a way to utilize the island. Of course, they were the only two classes who lived on the island as building restrictions were high and unaffordable to the majority of citizens from the other classes.

The Loradians had their own island on the opposite side of the lake much further to the south of Zanchier. They were very much their own ruling government. They separated themselves hundreds of years before, electing their own governors. Their cities and people seemed to thrive like no other, but they were very selective as to who they let into their beautiful city. The process to live or even visit Loradin was an extensive one. And the only people to serve in government positions were those born and raised there. Even the Praxtingen, Bakrisian, and Carpasian classes that dwelt near Loradin were protected by the Loradian Government and seemed to fare better than the same classes on the opposite side of the lake. Those who lived near Loradin had no desire to leave, hearing the horror stories of daily life from those of their classes. Especially now since war had broken out.

The classes tended to stay in their own areas, not moving too far away or crossing over into another's city. You did have some of the lower classes who lived and worked in all the major cities of Zanchier, but the Zanchieths, Martans, and Loradians all tended to stay where they were born and raised, content with their lives.

Very few of the upper class wanted anything different for themselves, and therefore there was little unrest in most of the families. Unfortunately for Harper's parents, she had an adventurous side. She wanted more than the boring, easy, life of her Martans-bred family. She wanted to see things outside of Martanzia and go places. That was how she had met Wilkins.

Wilkins had been born into the Praxtingen class. They were the middle working-class of Zanchier. Some of them made an excellent living, almost matching the Martans and Loradians if they were smart enough and worked hard enough. But most were happy with their status. They enjoyed life and were content with what they had. Harper had always been interested in this class of people and would often sneak out on weekends and go into the city for the day and just watch people. She traveled all over the city on different days, choosing who or what to watch that day.

One particular day she chose to go to the City-Edge Marketplace and watch people from the different classes intermingle with one another. That was when she first saw Wilkins Brinley. He had been a striking specimen indeed. It hadn't been just his appearance either. There had been something in his demeanor and the way he talked to and treated others. It appeared as though everyone was the same to him; all equal in their stature. It was the first time she had ever seen anyone treat others with equality. It had certainly made her think about how she behaved herself. After that encounter she conducted herself differently, much to the chagrin of her father.

She remembered that day so clearly, as though it were just yesterday. She and Wilkins were on opposite ends of the market square. He told her once he could feel someone watching him, and when he turned to locate who it was, he saw her. Their eyes locked and they both smiled ever so slightly at one another. Wilkins had stopped what he was doing and started across the square toward her. Harper did the same, following his lead. They met in the center, people bustling around them knocking them into one another. Wilkins looked down at her and simply said, "Hello", smiling brightly at her. She returned the sentiment in the same way and they both chuckled at their lack of articulation at a time like this. What felt like an eternity to them both had truly only been a matter of seconds before Wilkins father yelled for him and he had to leave.

He quickly said his name was Wilkins, and she quickly offered her own before he turned and walked back to his father, glancing over his shoulder to see her again. Harper stayed put where she was standing until he was no longer visible, both of them straining to see each other one last time as Wilkins and his father's cart disappeared around a corner.

She returned to that very market every chance she got for the next several months, hoping to see him again. One day she got lucky and there he was, not working, not talking with anyone, just searching the crowds. Searching for her.

After that day, the two of them were inseparable and planned days where they could meet as often as possible. Much to her chagrin and protesting, when Harper turned sixteen and could join the working class, her father decided she needed further education and shipped her to Bakrashan Scientific Academy. He said, *"to further her brilliant, scientific, mind."* Wilkins followed her there, taking up work in the city to be near her. Harper's father never knew of their relationship until she decided at the age of eighteen to introduce Wilkins to her parents. Their relationship had grown serious and he had asked her to marry him. Harper's father exploded over her wanting to marry below her own class. He disowned her that day and they had been at odds since then.

She and Wilkins married two years later after she finished academy. They had a small ceremony with his parents and some of their closest friends. Harper's mother came but watched from afar so her father wouldn't get word that she had gone. She and Wilkins had been so very happy. Years later, and after the birth of their first born, Bain, Wilkins parents retired to Loradin and Wilkins inherited his parents farm which had the rich ore-laden mine below. Harper's father became more interested in their lives after that and truly seemed to try to get to know Wilkins and his grandson.

Goodness. It was strange how just being back in this city brought back so many memories for her.

"Harper, are you okay?" Finn asked, watching her. His face was riddled with concern.

Harper, realizing that Finn had stopped the Voyager and had pulled to a stop by a small cafe, was stirred from her reverie and looked at her dear friend.

"Yes, I'm fine, Finn. Just lost in my memories. This place holds so many for me."

"Mostly good I hope?" he said, dismounting his Voyager.

"Yes, mostly good," she smiled and followed him, still taking in the sights and sounds, linking them with thoughts of the past.

"Since this is your old stomping ground and you've spent more time here, especially as a teenager, then tell me where we're going," Finn said, looking wearily at the large bustling city skyline and the immense amount of people on the streets.

"Why do you look so nervous, Finn?" Harper teased him as they walked toward the small cafe.

"I don't like cities. It's too hard to control the environment around you. I like my smaller towns because I can tell who's watching me and I can take care of situations quickly," he said with a lopsided grin.

"Believe it or not, you're probably not everyone's center of focus here," she teased again.

"Ha, ha, ha, Harper. I know that; I'm just uncomfortable is all."

Harper smiled up at him. Finn was a nice-looking man, and a rather large man at that. He knew his presence drew attention. She teased him about his thinking people noticed him, but they actually did. She just tried to make light of it to calm his nerves a bit. So, when needed, she teased him and made light of his fears just to calm him a bit and to get his mind off the fact that people actually were staring. Especially some of the women. Not to mention his Voyager was drawing some attention from the men as well. None of them approached Finn and his massive stature to ask questions about it, but they certainly gathered from afar staring at the thing and murmuring to themselves. Most of the self-proclaimed mechanics probably wished they could run home and start on one of their very own.

Most people of Zanchier traveled by many different forms. But none as archaic as Finn's Voyager. The upper classes traveled by MADS, -Matter Arranger Depositing Systems. Middle class still used animal or personal four-wheeled Modules, and the lower classes, if fortunate enough to own animals with carts used them, but most walked everywhere. If they lived and worked inside one of the larger cities they were fortunate enough to be able to have access to public transportation Modules.

"Finn, it's kind of hard to be incognito when you ride a thing like that. It draws a lot of attention. We may need to change avenues of transportation to avoid drawing attention to ourselves," Harper stated, feeling a bit edgy herself all of a sudden, noticing some people watching them both.

"I don't think it's my Voyager drawing all that attention, Harper. Even in your altered state and loose baggy pants and jacket, you're still a striking woman." Finn smiled at her blushing cheeks.

"Yeah, yeah, whatever. I doubt that's the case. But thank you for the compliment just the same," Harper said, turning to him and giving him a goofy grin. She stopped for a moment as her nerves began to get to her, "You don't think anyone recognizes me do you?" she asked, looking around nervously.

Finn grabbed her by the shoulders and turned her to look at him. "No way anyone here recognizes you. So, stop worrying," he reassured her in hushed tones.

Harper took a deep breath, nodded okay and they continued walking. They entered the small cafe and chose a table at the back of the room for as much privacy as possible. They would still speak in hushed tones and communicate through motions, because one never knew what sort of listening devices the government had stashed in the most unlikely of places.

The server left their water glasses, took their orders, and disappeared until it was time to bring the food.

"All right, Harp…" Finn stopped himself. "We need to think of another name for you. I can't keep using your given name or someone might just recognize you."

"You're right. Okay, names I can use?"

"I don't know…you're the girl, doesn't that sort of thing usually come easy to you?" Finn protested.

"Fine, ya' big baby." Harper breathed deeply. "How about Halsey? It's close enough but still different."

"All right, Halsey," Finn grinned, "How do we implement plan A?"

"After lunch here, we'll head to the Historical House and see about using one of the uplinks. I'll look up what the next event my parents are having, then we'll see about gaining employment at one of the catering, or entertainment companies."

"It's been a long time since I picked up a guitar, *Halsey*," Finn teased.

"Well, it's been a long time since I sang in public, Finn," she teased back.

"That probably wouldn't be a good idea. It would draw a lot of attention to yourself, not to mention, your parents, or others, may recognize your voice."

"My father doesn't even know I can sing. But you're right, mother does. So, to the kitchens it is."

"For you maybe. I can still play the guitar," he chuckled lowly.

Harper gave him a sarcastic look, and then a revelation hit her.

"You know, actually, that wouldn't be a bad idea. We could cover more areas of the house that way.

"Great. Besides, as you well know, I don't do well in tight, crowded spaces like busy kitchens full of tiny people running in all directions. That's a disaster waiting to happen for me."

Harper grinned at him and the pained look on his face at the thought of his description.

"We can look at sleeping accommodations after we figure out how long we have before the next event. We may have some down time to plan and figure it all out."

"Sounds good. I'll also get in touch with some contacts that I have in the entertainment industry and see if any of them know of any events planned. They usually have their fingers on the pulse of the area."

"Great. Here's to a successful mission, well laid plans, and to not having to use plan B," Harper said, raising her water glass to Finn who raised his in return.

"To well laid plans," Finn toasted back.

They ate their meal in relative silence as the next step in their plan played through both of their thoughts.

Chapter 8

Adda

Harper and Finn spent the next several weeks getting to know the people that were necessary for Harper's entry into her parent's home. She would enter under the guise of a kitchen servant for the catering company that her mother had booked for the party.

The great thing about the Social Events site for Port-Proud was that when listing the event of the hosting family, they also listed the catering company, the musicians, the decorators, the lighting, the clean-up crew, and just about anyone else in connection with the event. Everyone you could imagine got their listing. If it happened to get the title of Social Event of the season, everyone wanted their place in the spotlight as well.

She grabbed the dress she found at a local shop and put it on. She had to admit, she cleaned up nicely.

Finn almost dropped his coffee cup when she emerged from her room in the getup.

"Whoa, Harper. Aren't you just going for a catering position as kitchen staff?" he said, looking at her appearance. "With that dress and your hair like that, you may end up in more than you bargained for before the day's over."

To which, she replied, "I need to make sure I get on that crew. If not, I'll hit the next business listed, then the next, until I get a job. You need to be prepared for anything, Finn. You know that."

"Yeah, but I still think you're over doing it a bit with that dress," he said with raised eyebrows. Harper smiled sweetly and grabbed the heavy winter wrap that went with the dress and left.

Thirty minutes later, Harper walked into *Proud as Punch Catering* with her best face forward.

"Hi, my name is Halsey Barton, and I was wondering if you were hiring extra people for the Winterfest Event next weekend at the Fenore Estate?" She smiled sweetly at the pimply-faced young man behind the counter, who almost tripped over his own feet when she walked in wearing the slightly tight dress with the low-cut bodice.

"Uh…ye…yes ma'am. I believe the owner is looking for a few extra hands for the event. Can you just give me one minute, Ms. Barton? I'll be back in a flash," he said, backing slowly through the doorway, watching her as he went, smiling from ear to ear. Harper wiggled her fingers at him and smiled brightly, almost making him trip again.

When he left the room, she snickered uncontrollably at the poor guys reaction to her role-play.

"Hello, may I help you, Miss?" came a male voice from behind her. Harper smiled brightly before turning around to face the man.

"Hello, Sir," Harper said sweetly once again. "I was just curious to know if you needed extra help on the Fenore Event next weekend."

The slightly, older, somewhat attractive man, looked over her appearance with an appreciative glance. "My dear, I think you're a might over-qualified for this position. I'm hiring kitchen staff. You look like you belong on a stage somewhere."

"Well, that's awfully kind of you to say, but I'm afraid I don't have a lick of talent in anything other than the service department," she sighed ever so slightly.

The man cleared his throat and adjusted the knot in his tie, "Well," he squeaked out, and tried speaking again. "Well, Ms. Barton, is it?"

"Just call me Halsey, Sir," she beamed.

"I *am* in need of some help for the event. You can have the job if you think you really want it," he said, looking over her appearance again.

"Yes, of course I do, and thank you so much," she said, walking toward him and offering him her hand in a petite shake. "Thank you ever so much. When shall I report for my first day?" she asked.

"Why don't you just show up here at the shop the day before the event and I'll give you a run through of your duties. I think you'll catch on rather quickly," he smiled at her.

"Well, all right then. Thanks again, and I promise, you won't be disappointed." Harper grinned sweetly again, throwing her wrap around her shoulders, and turning to leave, smiling at him over her shoulder as she left the shop. "Ta now," she wriggled her fingers at him as she walked through the door.

"I'm certain I won't," the man said loudly after her, clearing his throat again as he watched her saunter out of his shop and onto the streets, disappearing into the crowds of people.

Finally, outside, Harper dropped the sweetness act.

"Step one, done. Now, for step two," she smiled as she made her way back to the weekly rentable apartment that she and Finn had rented for their stay in Port-Proud.

When she walked through the door and kicked off the offensive heels, Finn appeared from another room.

"Well, how did it go?"

"You have to ask?" she said grinning broadly.

"Now, Halsey," he said, getting used to the name, "what did you do to those poor fellas over at that catering shop."

"Not a thing. All I did was smile and be as sweet as the punch they are likely serving at the party," she said, disappearing into her room to change out of the confining dress.

Finn collapsed onto the sofa and waited for her return.

"So, what now," he asked in a raised voice.

"Now," she yelled back, "we find out what my kids look like because I haven't seen them in five years, and I'm pretty certain that their looks have changed quite a lot since they've grown."

"Good point. Do you think they will even be at the party?"

"Yes. Mother was always insistent that I was at her parties as one of the hosts, and I had to attend every soiree' that she ever threw. I had to dress and act the part of the proper socialite princess." Harper finished the sentence as she entered wearing some jeans and a loose-fitting cotton shirt.

Finn grinned, "There's the Harper I know," he stated in reference to her attire.

She grinned at him and plopped down next to him, grabbing a pillow, and wrapping her arms around it.

"I can't picture you playing a princess at all, for anyone or anything," Finn said, trying to capture the image in his mind of her in a puffy ball-gown.

"If you had seen my acting skills a little while ago, you wouldn't doubt that I was capable of anything that concerned acting," she giggled at the face he made.

"Well then, Princess Harper," he said in an animated voice, "what would your highness wish of me now?" He bowed slightly from his position on the couch.

Harper laughed at him as she batted him with the pillow in her hands. This was the playful side of Finn she hadn't seen for a while. Of course, the last time she spent this much time with him was when he had helped her escape and trained her to not only defend herself, but to fight like a man.

"All right, back to the seriousness of it all," she said, straightening up and sitting back against the cushions.

"How am I going to find out what my kids look like, Finn?"

"We could always check public academy records. They all have to have academy identification tags to attend any public training facility. And each year the kids attend, they take a new photograph."

"How do you know this stuff?" she asked quizzically.

Finn stopped for a minute before answering. "My kids attended Port-Proud Academy for the Advanced and Gifted," he stated, as the memories came flooding back in.

"Finn, I'm so sorry. That was a stupid question. I should have realized..."

"No, Harper, it isn't your fault. It's just that it is still really fresh in my mind. I can't wait to get my hands on the guy who ordered their execution. He's going to regret ever even hearing my name."

Harper patted her friend's hand, knowing nothing she said or did could comfort the pain the man had experienced over the years at the hands of corrupt government officials.

Finn sat up, shaking off the feeling of woe that had come over him.

"All right, Harper, let's take a look at all the academy listings and see if we can find a picture of your kids," he said, pulling a small device from his pack and pointing the projector eye at the adjacent blank wall.

"Where did you get that?" Harper asked in awe.

"Like I said, I know people." Finn grinned at her.

"Apparently you *really* know people," she stated, impressed that he could get his hands on such a device. A Palm-Cast was a small handheld device that cost thousands of Rhedons. It wasn't something most people just let you borrow. The only people to have them were mostly government officials such as the Zanchieths. Not even many of the Martans or Loradians possessed such technology.

They spent the next three hours searching the cities databases for all the academy listings, then set about finding those within close proximity to Everly-Sound. They chose academy's based on her children's ages and ran name searches for them. They only ran searches for first names, not wishing to draw attention to their intraweb activities by running Harper's last name just in case they flagged her children's last name against such activities.

It didn't take long for the Palm-Cast to locate one Bain Brinley age fifteen, Seadon Brinley age thirteen, and Wynne Brinley age eleven. There were several other children with the same first names but different surnames. The faces staring back at her were of strangers. The only one of them that looked somewhat the same was Bain. Only now he was like a carbon copy of his father Wilkins when he was around the same age.

Harper sat and stared at the images looking back at her, tears beginning to form in her eyes.

"I've missed so much, Finn," she said, her voice quivering with emotion as she swiped at the tears slowly streaking her cheeks. "They're almost grown."

Finn sat and rubbed Harpers back with one hand in a gesture of comfort, "I'm sorry, Harper. But at least they're alive and they look well. The oldest boy is even at the Academy for Advanced and Gifted learning, and the middle is in Future Airmen of Zanchier."

Harper could only shake her head in agreement. She looked at their faces, trying to find a resemblance between them and place each of them with the memories she had stored in her mind. She took a deep breath to steady her nerves and began to read their files. It listed their interests, strengths, fields of study, grades, and parents or guardians. She looked at her parent's names, under which it showed extended family. Wilkins Brinley and Harper Fenore Brinley were listed as deceased parents of all children. Also listed was someone named Adda.

Harper looked at the name, but it gave no other information. No age or anything. Maybe she was a long-lost relative who had been found? Why then wouldn't it give a last name?

"Finn, there's a name here I don't recognize but they're listed as a relative."

"What's the last name?"

"It doesn't give one, just a first name."

"They usually only list pre-academy children with first names. Once they attend primary academy a file will be created."

"Are you sure? Where would my mother have gotten a baby. Surely she didn't have a late-life pregnancy since I disappeared."

Harper froze for just a moment as a thought came to her mind, "Finn, are you certain about the government listing toddler aged children with first names only?"

"Yes. I think it has something to do with whether or not they ever attend an academy. Some children never do, you know. But that is mostly the Carpasian and Bakrisian class level. Why?" Finn questioned as he looked at Harper's frozen position and blank stare.

"Harper, are you all right?"

"She's mine," she said numbly.

"Who's yours?" Finn asked, unsure of what she meant.

"Adda," she barely mumbled.

"Do you mean the listed first name in the kids files?" he asked her, confused. "How could she be yours, Harper?"

"I was pregnant when they came and took me to Vasalage and ripped my other three children from my arms. The baby came one month prematurely, and they told me that it had died." Harper turned tear filled eyes to Finn. "The child listed as Adda. She has to be my baby. The one they told me died. Why would they do that?" she began to grow angry as her mind wheeled around her. "Why not at least tell me that the baby had survived?" She stood and began to pace the room.

Finn just watched her work through her recent discovery that she had another daughter. One who never knew her mother at all. He sat waiting for Harper to lose it, and he would be there to help her pick up the pieces once more. Only Harper never broke down, her anger grew, and she paced faster as the workings of her mind thought about the plan to see her children that now included one more. One who wouldn't know her. Her other children wouldn't know her either because of the dyes, toners, and digital scanning that she had done to hide her identity. Now, she wanted so badly to change her appearance back to one that her children might remember. She was already almost a stranger to them. She would be even more so if they couldn't recognize anything about her as their mother. And little Adda; she was a complete stranger to her. She would want nothing to do with Harper and certainly wouldn't want to leave the safety of her grandparent's home to go far away with a stranger. Even if her older siblings chose too. Harper was beginning to second guess her decision to contact her kids.

"Finn, what if this is all a big mistake?" she asked, stopping her pacing, and looking at her friend.

"I know why you're rethinking this, Harper. But they are your children. You didn't leave them. They were taken from you. They have as much right to know you as you do them."

"I know, I know, you're right, but I didn't realize Adda was alive. That changes things just a bit. She doesn't know me, Finn. That could make things very difficult."

"What do you want to do, Harper? Do you want to call the whole thing off?" Finn asked, watching her closely.

"Yes. NO! Ah…I just don't know," she said, planting herself on the couch, her elbows resting on her knees and her hands covering her face in frustration. She took several deep breaths and sat thinking.

"I need my kids, Finn. I don't care what happens to me, but I need to see them, at least one last time. Even if they choose to stay with my parents, at least I know they will be well taken care of there."

"All right then. Let's get this plan organized so you can't fail," Finn stated resolutely.

Chapter 9

Winterfest

"Today's the day, Finn," Harper stated nervously, tying her long hair back into a ponytail, and donning the uniform that the owner of *Proud as Punch* had given to her. She had showed up at the shop early yesterday morning with a different attitude than when she had gotten the job. The owner was a bit surprised and deflated by the change in her demeanor but decided to ignore it and move on. He desperately needed extra help with an event as large as the Fenore's Winterfest Social.

Harper's job fortunately was to serve drinks. She was to peruse the crowds with a tray of beverages. This was perfect for her. She could easily search for her kids while she worked this position.

Finn had gotten in with the band. He knew the manager personally. They were closely tied and even agreed to have someone as backup should Finn have to suddenly depart for the rest of the event. Harper was learning that Finn was heavily connected almost everywhere he went. She hadn't even had any real friends her whole life while growing up. The only person she really ever connected with had been Wilkins. She had made acquaintances since she had been on the run from the government, but no close friendships. None except for Finn. Harper didn't know what she would do without him. He had been invaluable to her, and willing to help her any way she needed without question or ulterior motives. Finn had never once tried to make a move on her. She was pretty sure he didn't feel that way for her and she was glad of it. Finn was indeed a catch for any other woman, but until Harper knew without fault that Wilkins was dead, she would forever hold out hope of his return. She was certain that Finn knew she felt this way and was glad that he respected her enough to treat their relationship as such. Finn was like an uncle to her, a beloved favorite uncle who doted on and spoiled her.

Harper shook herself free of her wandering thoughts and tried to stay focused on the task at hand. It was still eight hours before the event started and was in full swing. The servers would spend the whole morning packing the trucks with food and drink, serving trays, servers towels, which they carried over their arms to be ready for unexpected spills, punch bowls, dry ice, and a multitude of other items necessary for such an event.

Finn wondered into the small kitchen of their apartment.

"Morning, Halsey," he grinned at her.

"Morning, Mr. guitar player," she replied with a smile. "I'm already a bundle of nerves, Finn. I don't know how I am ever going to get through tonight, especially if I actually get to see one of my kids."

"You'll be fine, Harper. Just remember to stay calm, no one will know it's you, and right now, that's a good thing."

"Okay," she turned to face him, stood on her tiptoes, and planted a kiss on his cheek, "wish me, luck," she said, grabbing her jacket.

"No luck needed, Harper. I had a word with the Creator," he said crossing his arms over his chest and leaning against the cabinet.

"Well, let's hope he's listening today. See you tonight," she said, speeding out the door with a wave of her hand.

Harper reached the catering shop just in time for the brief staff meeting that was required for large events. They spent the next twenty-minutes going over the layout of the Fenore mansion, each server getting a certain area to tend to for the evening. They also each had a fifteen-minute, scheduled break, every two hours for necessity and light snacks. A rotation schedule was passed out to those paired together for the evening and they were given explicit instructions that under no circumstances were they to interact with the guests in any other way than their service jobs required.

Harper wondered if she would be able to steal a chat with Bain should she get the opportunity? Of course, at any given time during the night, she could abandon her service position and do whatever she wanted. The job wasn't what was important here. She wished she had thought about that sooner and had brought along a disguise with her.

The Module was loaded with all the supplies, and all the servers were to meet at the Fenore mansion at three o'clock to prepare for the party and set up. This early arrival would give her the added opportunity to maybe spot her kids. She wasn't sure yet about letting her parents know that she was here. She didn't want to involve them and possibly cause them problems in the future. The less they knew right now the better. Besides, her mother would likely make a scene by fawning over her and blowing her cover.

Harper didn't have transportation to Everly-Sound, so she caught a ride with one of the other women who was working as a server for the party.

"Thanks a lot for the ride. Public Modules take too long to make the rounds. I probably would have ended up being late," Harper said, making small talk with the older woman.

"No problem. I borrowed a friends Module today so I wouldn't have to take public transport. I get it. By the way, the name's Moira."

"Moira," Harper nodded, "I'm Halsey."

"Nice to meet you, Halsey. How long have you lived in Port-Proud?"

"Just a few weeks," Harper replied, hoping Moira wouldn't get too personal.

"I've lived here for twenty-years now. I moved here from Terra Valley, just below the Xantifal Mountains on the northern side of Bakrashan. I'm Bakrisian. There wasn't much work for me back in my village, so I decided to try my luck here. It's been a pretty decent living. Better than I would have had back home anyway. Where do you hail from?" she asked, glancing briefly at Harper.

"Treeline Valley," she lied.

"So, you're Bakrisian as well?" she asked curiously.

"Uh, yeah," Harper answered short.

"What did your parents do there?"

"My father ran one of the merchant shops."

"Really, which one? I might know him." Moira asked; excitement written across her features.

Think, Harper, what to say now. "I doubt it since you've been gone for twenty years. He just acquired the store about ten years back," Harper said, hoping she believed the story. She was beginning to wonder if riding the public Module would have been safer.

"Oh, yeah. You're probably right about that."

Moira kept talking about anything and everything, and by the time they reached Everly-Sound and the Fenore Estate thirty-minutes later, Harper almost ran from the car. She had never encountered anyone who talked as much as Moira. She would have to make sure she caught a ride back with Finn when the event ended. She couldn't handle another car ride with the ever-chatty Moira.

When she walked into the kitchen, she recognized some of her parent's staff members and her heart felt as though it would jump out of her chest it was beating so hard. She avoided any run ins with them just in case they might recognize her. How was she going to get through tonight? She took a deep breath, grabbed some of the table settings and walked into the large hall. The room was massive, with a grand, wide, staircase on the far end leading to a second-floor level. The center of the floor was open, and tables were scattered rather tightly around the edges of the room, about sixty tables in total, all seating about ten people. Other catering staffers soon joined her in the room, all busy with setting up the formal dining settings for over six hundred people. Harper had never been on this side of an event before. It was interesting to see what it took to throw one of these things. The work that went into it and the people it took to make it all happen was amazing. Something she had never had to worry about being on the other side.

On the far end of the room, next to the large staircase was the stage for the musicians and performers. Harper looked up to see the band beginning to set up their equipment. She spotted Finn and he spotted her. They glanced at one another then set about their duties.

Harper could hear someone running and heard yelling on the second floor just at the staircase. As she glanced up, she saw her mother dressed in one of her beautiful gowns, calling out to a young boy.

"Seadon Brinley, you stop right there this instant, young man."

Harper's breath seized in her chest as she watched the two interact just across the room from her, mid-way up the staircase.

"Grandmother, why do I have to go to this stupid party anyway?" Seadon protested, stopping as instructed.

"Because it is what good hosts do. And as a member of this family, you are one of the hosts, you know that. We go over this every time we have a party," she said firmly, yet lovingly.

"Exactly; we have too many parties!" he protested, pulling at the constraining tie.

"Stop fidgeting with your tie, Seadon and go find Bain and Wynne, and make sure everyone is dressed. And find your suit jacket as well. I best not catch you again without it," she said firmly but with a smile to finish the scolding.

"Yes, Grandmother," Seadon said defeated, as he drudgingly walked up the stairs to do as he was told.

Harper couldn't take her eyes from Seadon. One of her children was standing just forty feet or so away.

"Halsey…Halsey," came the firm use of her fake name. Harper jumped, looking at the owner of *Proud as Punch,* who was staring at her.

"Yes, sir?" she replied.

"You need to see to your work. Whatever transpires amongst the family members is none of your business, understand?" he said strictly.

"Yes sir, sorry," she said, turning and glancing up one last time to watch Seadon climb the staircase as she slowly left the room.

Gracelynn Fenore noticed the exchange and the way the young woman watched Seadon before exiting the ballroom. She seemed vaguely familiar to her, but she was sure she had never seen the woman before.

Finn noticed that Gracelynn Fenore continued to look at the door that Harper exited through. She shook her head and turned back up the staircase and disappeared. Surely, she didn't recognize Harper. Finn didn't see how she could have. Harper looked very little like herself, but her mannerisms and movements could very well remind her mother of who she was. Not to mention the way Harper was staring at them. She needed to keep her head and be careful or she was going to give herself away. He would have to get word to Harper somehow that she needed to straighten up and steer clear of Gracelynn, or she could cause Harper problems.

Two hours later the party was in full swing and Harper was one of the servers to work the large ballroom. She was also told to make sure the entertainers had water to drink during their performance.

"Water only, Miss Barton, do you understand? We certainly do not need a bunch of drunken musicians at tonight's event."

"I understand, Sir," Harper smiled sweetly as he turned to instruct another employee. Was it just her he talked down to? Maybe the man was still angry that she wasn't the same woman whom he thought he had hired last week?

Harper went to the kitchen, grabbed some bottles of water, and headed to the stage as the musicians were just finishing their first set. She passed out the bottles to everyone, finishing off with Finn last so they could briefly chat.

"I didn't know you could play so well, Finn," she admired.

"I happen to be a man of many talents," he smirked back.

"So I'm learning," she smiled as she turned to leave.

"Hey," he said to catch her attention, stooping down to speak quietly. "Be careful. You were a little too obvious, and you captured Gracelynn's attention."

"Thanks, momentary slip up." She nodded and turned to work the crowd.

A half-hour later, guests began filtering into the ballroom as the dinner hour was about to begin. The entertainment changed to orchestra music to play softly while the guest's dined. After which the band Finn was with would resume playing dance music for another two hours. The party would end with a show of skyrockets exploding in an array of colors to light the night sky.

Harper knew what would happen next. She had avoided seeing her parents as much as possible, and fortunately they tended to mingle with the more prominent people on the extremely large second floor balconies. But now her father, Derek Fenore, would make a speech before they dined amongst all their guests.

Derek Fenore stood with glass in hand, toasting his guests as Harper watched from a few tables away. She filled drinking glasses, working her way to her parent's table where all four of her children were now seated. She took in each one of their appearances. Especially the littlest who did indeed appear to be around five years old. Her little Adda, then her beautiful Wynne, now all of eleven years old. Beside her sat Seadon, and then Bain. Goodness, how he resembled Wilkins when he was sixteen, the first time she had laid eyes on him.

Now that her father had finished his speech, she had to fill the glasses at their table. Her nerves were taught as bow strings and she tried to keep her head down and turned away from Gracelynn Fenore. Her mother hadn't seemed to pay her anymore mind, but she still needed to be cautious. As she walked around the table filling the glasses of apparently some of her parent's closest friends or business colleagues, she would steal glances at her beautiful children.

"Young Seadon, I hear you're an excellent pilot all ready," boomed one of the men at the large twenty-seat, rectangular table.

"Yes sir," Seadon answered, "I'm going to be the youngest pilot ever to fly the new airships across Zanchier."

The table erupted with laughter at his confident answer.

Harper smiled to herself. Seadon always had been a strong-willed, hard-headed child who knew exactly what he wanted early on.

Gracelynn Fenore watched the young woman from beneath her lashes as she walked cautiously around the table filling all the glasses. She noticed that she seemed to watch the children quite frequently. She seemed so familiar to her, but she just couldn't place her finger on who she was. She must know her from somewhere.

As Harper made the rounds, she soon came to her father who paid her no mind whatsoever thank goodness. Then her mother, whom she tried her hardest not to make eye contact with. As she poured the liquid into the glass, she could feel her mother's eyes on her.

"Thank you, my dear," Gracelynn said. Harper stiffened a bit. Her mother never told servers thank you. At least she had never heard her do so in all the years of events as a child and an adult.

Harper nodded and slightly bowed, never making eye contact. She moved on to Bain who sat right next to her mother. He looked up at her and smiled as she poured into his glass. She stood a bit too long and stared. She knew that, but she couldn't help herself. She nodded, smiled back, and moved on. All the while she could feel Gracelynn's eyes on her while the rest of the table chatted and laughed at things her children would say in reply to questions they were asked. As she filled each of her children's glasses, she lingered as long as she could without drawing attention to herself. Seadon, bold and fearless, relishing the attention of his interested party. Her beautiful freckle-faced Wynne, with her striking red hair, just like hers. Then there was the beautiful, petite blond who sat next to Wynne. Just a hint of red touched her curls that bobbed up and down as she moved.

"Thank you very much, lady," the sweet smile and joyful blue eyes looked up at her.

Harper's breath caught in her throat, as she looked at the precious girl. She wanted so badly to scoop her into her arms and never let go.

"You're very welcome, young one," she managed to say with a steady voice and a grin. She quickly finished her job of filling glasses at the table and hurried back to the kitchen. She put down the pitcher and tray and tried to find a place to calm her shaking hands and steady her nerves. She wanted to cry, to scream at the top of her lungs at the injustice done to her and her family, over nothing but simple greed of the government. She ran out the side kitchen door and outside the house, finding an unoccupied bench far from the crowds. It was her time for a break anyway, so no one should notice her missing. Little did she know that Gracelynn had seen her hasty departure and had excused herself from the table and followed where she had gone.

Gracelynn slowly approached the young woman who sat on the bench, bent forward with her elbows resting on her knees, and her face in her hands. She was certainly built the same as Harper. Perhaps a bit more muscular than Harper had been, but there was no mistaking her pose. When Harper was younger, when she would get upset, she always sat the same way. Shielding her face, pain, and emotions from the world around her.

"Harper?" came her mother's voice from behind her. She stiffened, unsure what to do or say.

Without looking back, she simply said, "No ma'am, my name's Halsey Barton."

"Do you honestly think I wouldn't recognize my own daughter, even with the changes you've made," Gracelynn said, stopping in front of her.

Harper looked up into the trembling, tear-streaked face of her mother. Harper stood and cautiously tried to explain.

"Mother," she said as her voice began to crack, "You shouldn't be here, it's dangerous."

"I thought you were dead," her mother said, placing both hands on her cheeks.

Harper tried to back away, pulling her mother's hands away. "Listen to me, Mother. You can't be here. I'm running from the people who had me imprisoned. I can't explain right now, there are too many people," she said, whispering and glancing around for eavesdroppers.

"Meet me right back here directly after the sky-rocket show begins. I want to hear what happened to you," Gracelynn said. After hugging Harper fiercely, she squared her shoulders, putting the acting career she had before marriage back into play. She resumed the gracious hostess facade, looked at Harper in the eyes once more and went back inside.

Harper collapsed onto the bench. Her frazzled nerves were unable to take many more surprises.

Chapter 10

Vassalage

"Finn, my mother knows. She recognized me," Harper said, as she furnished more water to the band during another break.

"I thought she was on to you. What now? Do we need to leave?" he asked her, ready to bolt if needed.

"No, she said to meet her after the party, outside the kitchen."

"You sure that's a good idea?"

"We'll see," she said, turning to get back to her job. She walked around the ballroom watching her children interact with the other guests. As she picked up empty glasses from revelers exchanging them for filled ones, she had the opportunity to watch her children dance together, laugh with each other, and visit with some other children who were obviously their friends. She also noticed another group of youths in attendance that appeared to be at odds with Bain and his friend called Kreelie.

By nine pm the sky-rocket show was scheduled to begin and would last for half an hour, after which the Winterfest event would come to an end as people would begin to say their goodbyes. While the guests enjoyed the show, all service individuals hired for the night would tend to cleaning-up whatever area they had served in for the evening.

As the hour was reaching fifteen minutes before nine, the guests began converging outside on the lawn, sitting upon chairs or one of the hundreds of heated blankets scattered across the massive, blue, snow-dusted lawn.

Harper walked through the kitchen, laid the serving tray and empty glasses on the counter, and walked out the staff door to the partially hidden, outside courtyard to wait where her mother had asked her to. She stood outside and watched the light show high above the mansion as pieces of the sky-rocket explosions scattered across the night-sky. Suddenly, she felt a searing pain in the back of her head as everything went dark.

Harper's head ached horribly and opening her eyes to the harsh light made it hurt even worse. She had no idea where she was. She lay there, trying to get over the nausea she felt and the dizziness that accompanied her headache.

"Well, hello, Harper. So glad you could join us here back at home. I must say, we've missed you," came a familiar sickening voice.

"No…please tell me I'm not…" Harper grew even more nauseous when she realized she was back in her prison cell at Vassalage.

"Of course you are. Did you really think we wouldn't find you? Even though, we really thought you dead. Of course, you did quite a good job with your disguise, and you might have gotten away with it if you hadn't have let your heart over-rule your head," Commander Raif Martray stated in a cocky, slippery tone.

"Why can't you people just leave me and my family alone?" she eked out through gritted teeth, rubbing the back of her neck while she spoke from her sitting position on the cot.

"You never finished the job we charged you with, Harper. A deal's a deal."

"I never made a deal with anyone. You ripped me from my husband, my kids, even my parents."

Martray's tone became harsh and more sinister, making Harper look up, her vision still a bit blurry. "Details aren't important Harper. Point is, you need to finish the job."

"I'm sorry, but due to a splitting headache and near impossible vision, not to mention the nausea and dizziness, I'm a little incapacitated at the moment."

"Yes, well, I'll take care of the brute who was stupid enough to hit our prized scientific genius on the head. You just get better, Hmmm? Anything I can get you to help speed the wellness along?"

"Sure. How about a key and a ride home?" she said, a sarcastic tone in her answer.

Commander Martray smiled appreciatively at her resolve. "Perhaps in due time, when you finish our little project."

Harper tried to stand but fell backward onto the bed again as dizziness and nausea took her body over in overwhelming intensity.

Martray looked dismayed at her incapacitation. "Guard," he yelled, "get her some soup, bread, water, and some pain medicine. And I want the two idiots who did this to her taken out and executed for their stupidity."

"Yes, Commander," the voice stammered a bit in answer.

Harper lay there wondering what that was all about. The commander had no love for her that was certain. Surely he was only concerned with her health in respect to how quickly she could get back to work on their weapon. It hurt horribly to think right now. All she could do was rest and try to sleep. The guard soon returned with the food ordered by Martray, and Harper begrudgingly ate the soothing hot broth, warm bread, and drank the water, taking the pain medicine with it. After finishing the meal, she laid back on her cot and let sleep claim her for the next eight hours.

It was 9:45 and people were filing out of the Fenore home in droves. Finn walked the grounds of the mansion, yelling for Halsey. He asked the crew she had worked with that night if anyone had seen her.

"She went to the kitchen with a tray of glasses but, I haven't seen her since," said one of the staff girls.

"Do you know what time that was?"

"Maybe forty-five minutes to an hour ago."

"Thanks," Finn said walking off to search the kitchen.

He walked through the large area, peeking into any door or around any corner available. He noticed the door leading outside and his gut twisted just a bit. Didn't Harper tell him earlier that she was supposed to meet her mother outside the kitchen?

He walked out the door which turned and led to a small seating area. He looked around carefully, hoping to see some kind of clue.

"Excuse me, who might you be?" came the questioning voice of a woman.

Finn turned slowly and found himself looking into the face of Gracelynn Fenore.

"No one ma'am. Just one of the musicians needing some air."

"Couldn't you get that by the front side-door where your Mod is parked and being loaded?"

"Yes, I suppose I could. Excuse me ma'am, I'll just be going," Finn said, starting to walk away.

"Are you a friend of Harper's?" she quickly asked.

Finn stopped in his tracks. He turned to look at her, unsure what, or if, he should answer.

"Do you know where she is? She was supposed to meet me here during the sky-rocket show, but even though I keep searching for her, I can't find her. Did she get frightened and leave?"

Finn sighed heavily and looked at Gracelynn. She seemed sincere enough, besides, he didn't know where Harper was anyway. "I am a friend, but I can't find her either."

"She told me it was dangerous, and that I shouldn't be talking to her."

"Did anyone else overhear you talking with her, or did you tell anyone else you saw her?" Finn questioned.

"What is all this about anyway? Who would want to take Harper, or harm her?" Gracelynn asked, growing anxious.

"You didn't answer my question, Mrs. Fenore," Finn said, staring at her.

"Only my husband. I don't think anyone overheard us, but perhaps they did."

"Did you tell him you were meeting her out here?"

"Well, yes. I figured he would want to come as well, but he said if he disappeared before certain business associates left, he'd never hear the end of it. He told me to come alone and he would see to the guests and meet up with us after. Please, if you know where she is, tell her I really wish to speak with her."

"I don't know where she is, Mrs. Fenore. I haven't seen her for a few hours now. I'm growing concerned. I think she may have been taken prisoner again."

"By whom, and why?" Gracelynn asked, confused.

"We're not completely sure, but we believe the government, ma'am. They're trying to make her build a weapon for them."

"Good heavens!" Gracelynn exclaimed, sitting on the bench. "Is that why she changed her appearance so drastically?"

"Yes. She's been running for the last three years."

"What can I do to help?"

"Nothing ma'am. She didn't want you to get involved for fear of you and the kids getting hurt. She only came tonight to see her kids again. To talk to them and let them know she is still alive. But I wouldn't say anything to them yet. Not until I can find her."

"Yes, I understand. Thank you for being there for her. I just wish there were more that I could do. Please, if you find her, could you let me know?"

"I can try, but just coming back here may have gotten her captured again, so I don't think it's safe."

Gracelynn stood, unsure what else to say. She looked at the man standing in front of her, shook her head in understanding, and walked past him into the house without another word. Who could have overheard her conversation with Derek? Perhaps Derek mentioned something to someone else. She would ask him tonight before bed after the children were asleep and everyone else had left. How could this happen again? How could she find and lose her daughter all in the same night?

Harper woke much later to the smell of food. Commander Martray had never been this considerate of her before. Sure, they had fed her, but not the good stuff she had last night and the eggs, toast, sausage, and coffee she saw on the table in her room this morning. Not to mention they had also brought her more pain medicine. She ate the food, knowing she needed to keep up her strength, but she was going to nurse the headache and nausea thing for as long as she could.

She wondered where Finn was, and if he even knew she had been abducted once again. Would he be able to break her out a second time? Would she just have to resolve to build the deadly weapon? Even if she did, would they really let her go to resume the life she had before all of this? She seriously doubted it. Besides, she had already lost so many years.

Commander Martray returned to her cell three days later, ready for her to commit to his request.

"All right, Harper, you've had three full days to recover, with adequate medicine and food. It's time you get back to work on our project."

"I don't exactly have a choice do I?" she stated, standing, and following him and the two guards from her locked room.

"No, you don't. But we *would* all get along much better if you'd hurry and finish it."

"We'd get along a lot better if you weren't holding me prisoner here against my will."

"Tsk, tsk, now, Harper. Prisoner is such a strong word. You're simply my guest until I grow tired of you," he said, stopping in the hall and turning to look at her. "And if you wish to see your children ever again, or your parents, I suggest you cooperate, quickly," he said, turning abruptly and walking away as the guards pushed her forward behind him.

Finn was unable to find Harper anywhere and decided to talk with Bain Brinley, the oldest of her four children. Perhaps she had said something to him last night that may lead Finn to what had happened to her. Finn believed the boy was old enough to be able to handle the truth.

Finn went to Port-Proud Academy for the Advanced and Gifted, and hung around waiting to see if he could catch Bain alone. Fortunately, he was able to do just that when Bain went outside to sit at some tables for lunch. There wasn't anyone else around seeing as how it was still a bit cool outside. Bain had his uplink with him and was very interested in something on it.

"Bain Brinley?" Finn said, without sitting down just yet.

Bain looked up at him, hit a button on his uplink, and closed the lid. "Yeah, I'm Bain."

"My name is Finn Mobley. I would like to speak with you a minute if I can?"

"Sure. Should I know you? Wait a minute, you're the guitar player from the party last night," Bain stated, eyeing the large man who just sat down across from him.

"Yes, I am, but you don't know me. I am, however, a friend of your mother's," Finn said cautiously, looking at Bain.

Bain sat motionless for a moment just looking at Finn, "My mother's alive? I knew it!"

"Calm down now, Bain. We don't want to draw unnecessary attention to ourselves."

"Sorry, but I've been searching for her for months now. Where is she? Can I see her?"

"Well, your reply tells me one thing, that she didn't talk to you last night."

"What? What do you mean? My mother was at our event last night?"

"Yes. She posed as a server with the catering company so she could get in to see you and your siblings."

"I remember my mother and what she looked like. I didn't see her anywhere. Was she working in the kitchen or something?"

"No, she was actually the woman who served your drinks and meals at your table last night."

"No way. I didn't notice her. Why didn't she say anything?" Bain asked, growing a bit upset.

"Bain calm down. I need you with a clear head and I need you to pay attention. She had to change her appearance so that the people who were after her wouldn't recognize her. They held her prisoner for the first two years forcing her to build a weapon for them. She escaped and has been running for the last three years trying to get back to you and your siblings. Last night, she was supposed to meet your grandmother outside the kitchen during the fireworks, but Harper never showed up. Your grandmother doesn't know what happened. I was just hoping that she may have said something to you."

"No, she never did. What do you think happened? Can you find her?"

"I don't know Bain, but I'm going to try. I'm going to give you an e-link where you can get in touch with me should you need anything, all right?"

"Yeah, sure. Here's mine," Bain said, handing him a piece of paper with the scribbled e-link as Finn handed his to Bain, carefully exchanging the addresses in case someone was watching them.

"I'll be in touch, Bain. And remember, tell no one we spoke or that your mother is alive. I am trying everything I know to do to find her," Finn said, standing to leave.

"I won't, and thanks, Mr. Mobley, for speaking to me and letting me know. It gives me hope."

"You can call me Finn, son." With that and a nod, Finn turned and left Bain sitting at the table.

Finn spent the next three days contacting everyone he knew that could be trusted and searched every government facility he could get access to, trying to find anything on Harper Fenore, Harper Brinley, or Halsey Barton. He found nothing.

"Come on Harper; where are you?" he said out loud as he watched the Palm-Cast fly through thousands of pieces of information in a matter of minutes. A message came across the Palm-Cast screen to his locked mailbox belonging to his alias. Only members of the old resistance had that e-link, and he hadn't talked to anyone or received anything through it in the last two years.

Finn opened the message which was encrypted with an old code used back in his resistance days.

"What do we have here, and from whom?" he wondered, working to decode the message.

It was an invitation for him to attend talks of rebuilding the resistance, but what was the most interesting part was the letterhead for which it came upon. It bore the seal of the Loradin government. Loradin had always been neutral in the wars of Zanchier, refusing to get involved or take sides. What could have happened to change their minds, he wondered?

Finn asked for a more public meeting and one in person with the sender of the message. He received a reply that his request was acceptable and was given a time and place for the meeting. Finn agreed, let the Palm-Cast finish its searches, and set about formulating a plan of escape, just in case the message was a trap.

The next morning, he got up, checked the result readings from the Palm-Cast which showed no news on the location of Harper, and set about getting ready for his lunch meeting with whoever had sent him the e-link.

Chapter 11

The Discovery

Bain Brinley sat by the large oak door listening intently to the conversation happening on the other side. The muffled sounds of raised voices was hard to make out, but he believed he could understand enough of the conversation and the subject matter.

Grandfather was discussing the recent appearance of his mother. Bain now knew she was alive somewhere, and he figured he would find her one day. She had beat him to it and had found them first but was taken from them again. He just wished he knew who his grandfather was talking to. Grandfather's office had an outside facing door which his business associates would come and go through, without having to enter through the main house.

If Bain ran to the window that faced the door entering grandfather's office, he could make out who he was talking to once the man left. But to do that he would have to forgo hearing the conversation, and that was really the important part.

Bain hunkered down as low to the keyhole as he could and peered inside, unable to really see anything. He looked around the hall to make sure no one was coming and pressed his ear to the keyhole.

"I've already done as you've asked of me. I cannot get further involved. If my family learns of what I've done, I could lose them all," his grandfather begged.

"You will do as told or you will most certainly lose them all," came the voice of the unknown man.

"How dare you threaten me in my own home!" grandfather challenged.

"It isn't a threat, Derek. It's a promise. We'll take your grandchildren and split them up, shipping them to wherever we choose. Then, I'll take your dear Gracie and do whatever

I so wish. I've always fancied her you know?" the voice stated in a sleazy way.

"I'll have you hanged for it! You will not touch another member of my family. It's bad enough that I had to turn Wilkins and Harper over to you. I won't do it again."

"But you already have," the voice slithered. "We apprehended Harper again the night of your Winterfest event. Thanks for telling us where and when to find her. You must really dislike that girl of yours."

"What goes on in my family is none of your business. What I did to Harper is for the greater good of everyone. This meeting is over. It's time for you to leave."

"Fine. Just remember what I said, Derek. You either cooperate with us, or you'll suffer the consequences."

Bain was frozen in disbelief for a few seconds. Did he hear his grandfather correctly? Surely it was a mistake. Bain stood and ran to his room to mull over everything he had just heard. He quickly sat at his desk, took some paper and a pencil, and began to record the conversation word for word before he forgot any of it. Perhaps if he saw it on paper it would make more sense.

Bain sat staring at the page before him. His grandfather had betrayed his own daughter and her husband, handing them both over to whoever he had been speaking to. Not only once, but twice for his mother. Because of him, Bain and his siblings could forever be torn from their mother and father. Would his mother be able to survive imprisonment again? Why would his grandfather do this? Bain didn't understand. Surely grandfather had major connections in the higher offices that would guarantee them protection. Not to mention the wealth he had that he could use for just such a thing.

Bain felt as though the weight of the world landed on his fifteen-year-old shoulders. This new information was one that he almost wished he hadn't heard. How would he be able to face his grandfather knowing what he did? And how would he ever find his mother again?

Bain's head was spinning with the information he just learned. He had to get out of the house, but he had to do so without running into his grandfather, because he wasn't sure what he would do or say if he saw him anytime soon.

Bain ran downstairs and out the front doors as quickly as possible, making his way across the front lawn, sprinting as quickly as he could toward Everly Lake. Once he got to the dock, he jumped into the small rowboat that they often had tied there and rowed as hard and as quickly as he could out toward the middle of the recently thawed lake. Thirty minutes had passed before he ran out of steam and collapsed into the bottom of the boat, unable to move another muscle.

Bain lay there in the boat, exhausted, confused, hurt, and angry. He screamed into the air at the top of his lungs, trying to release some of his frustrations. He lay in the boat as tears welled up in his eyes, crying for the loss of his family, the knowledge that his grandfather had betrayed all of them, especially his mother, and the loss of his innocence and his youth.

He lay there dealing with his grief for the next hour or so as the boat slowly rocked his grief-stricken mind and body until he felt numb. After his mind and body had no more to give, he rowed the boat back to the dock, tied it up, and instead of going into the house, he walked along the Lake's edge toward his friend Kreelie's house.

Would Kreelie understand? Should he even tell Kreelie about what he had discovered? Should Bain tell anybody? He was so confused, and he felt so alone.

It wasn't too much longer before Bain would be sixteen and he would be able to join the working class of Zanchier. Many benefits came with being an adult of the working class, privileges that would allow him to get away from his Grandparent's house. New graduates were granted small living quarters in an apprenticing community of their particular field of study, all bills paid, and a food stipend for the first year, until which time they had to have enough money saved to be able to move out and purchase their first starter home or apartment. With that kind of freedom, he could continue the search for his mother and possibly even tell grandmother what he had learned. But he wouldn't say anything until he was able to leave. Then, maybe he could take Seadon and Wynne with him. He could take care of them by himself. Besides, they were old enough to understand things and fend for themselves when it came to being able to be left alone at home. The only problem was that he would have to leave Adda.

Bain had a lot to consider and think about concerning his future and that of his siblings. One thing was for certain, he would find out more about what his grandfather had done, and why.

Bain reached Kreelie's back door which faced the lakeside and knocked. He could hear someone approaching. Kreelie opened the door in his usual jovial way.

"Hey, Bain, my buddy. What brings you by?" Kreelie said smiling, soon realizing that Bain was not himself. "Bain? What's wrong man?" Kreelie said stepping to the side as he ushered Bain through the door and inside.

"Kreelie, I need your help and I'm not sure where to start," Bain said, looking around nervously. "Is there somewhere we can talk in private?"

"Yeah, man. Just let me get my coat and boots and we can head out to the boathouse." Kreelie left him standing there to retrieve the items and returned soon, ready to step out into the wintry air.

The boys both walked to the boathouse in silence, their hot breath creating fog in the air as they breathed out. The weather was beginning to warm as spring was just around the corner, but the air still had a bite to it.

Once inside the boat house, Kreelie turned the thermostat up and set it to a comfortable temperature. Then he went to grab them both a cold drink and they each sat in one of the over-sized chairs in the room located in front of a large picture window overlooking Everly Lake.

Bain took a long drink of the cool liquid to coat his hoarse throat before beginning. He sighed heavily, unsure where to start.

"Bain? Man, are you all right? Did something happen to one of your sisters or your brother?" Kreelie questioned him, concerned for his friend. He had never seen Bain so upset before.

"Kreelie, you *have* to promise me not to tell a living soul what I am about to tell you. Not until I figure out what to do, Okay?"

"Word of honor, Bain. What's the problem?"

"You know how I've been searching for my mom for years now."

"Yeah, constantly. Did you find her? Is she okay?" Kreelie asked excitedly, but unsure whether she was alive based on Bain's mood.

"More like she found me."

"What? Bain, that's awesome, man!" Kreelie jumped up and began pacing the area in front of his chair.

"No, Kreelie, it isn't!" Bain snapped.

Kreelie stopped moving, his mood growing somber.

"Sorry for snapping at you, Kreelie. But I need you to just be quiet for a minute and listen until I'm finished talking."

"Okay, Bain. Finish." Kreelie sat down, more worried for his friend than ever before. Bain had never yelled at him like that in all the years that they had been friends.

"My mom showed up at my grandparent's house during the Winterfest event. She was posing as a server, only I didn't recognize her. She must have looked completely different, Kreelie."

"So, I probably saw her then?" Kreelie asked, scanning his memory through the faces he saw that night. "It's been a really long time since you last saw her, Bain. Don't feel bad just because you didn't recognize her," his friend comforted.

"Not different like that. I mean she had to change her entire appearance. I didn't recognize her at the party, and so I didn't really talk to her because she was one of the kitchen servants working for the catering company. Monday, after the party, this man showed up at the academy, and came and sat beside me at lunch. I went out to set at the outside tables with my uplink to be alone and do some more searches. He walked up, introduced himself, and said he wanted to talk about my mother. I didn't know what to think, but then he told me about my mom and wondered if she had contacted me at the party."

"Man, I miss everything. Figures I'd get sick Monday and miss academy," Kreelie said in aggravation. "Why did she change her appearance?" Kreelie questioned, this small detail bothering him.

"He said she had been held prisoner for the first two years and that someone was forcing her to build them a weapon. She escaped, and a friend helped her to change her appearance so they couldn't find her again. She's been on the run for the last three years."

"Man, that's intense," Kreelie stated.

"Yeah, but the worst part is that my grandfather had something to do with her being taken. And I think he also had something to do with my father's disappearance six years ago too."

"No way, man! Your granddad wouldn't do that. Would he?" Kreelie asked, shocked.

"I overheard him talking with someone in his office. I even wrote the conversation down and studied it to make sure what I heard was right. There is no mistaking what he said, Kreelie. My grandfather turned in his own daughter and son-in-law to save his own neck from something. He tore apart my family, Kreelie. Made orphans of his own grandchildren. He's been lying to us our entire lives."

"What about your grandmother? Do you think she knows too?"

"I don't know what to think, Kreelie. I don't know who to trust anymore."

"Well, what about your mom? Are you going to see her again?"

"I don't know, the man I spoke with said that she was missing again. He said he was looking for her."

"Are you sure this guy can be trusted?"

"Yeah, I think so. I think they took her again. Kreelie, I still remember what happened when I was ten. Men came into our house and dragged our mother outside. Then they came in and took all of us somewhere else. It was only a matter of hours before my grandfather came to collect us. I never thought that was strange before now, but how did he know where to find us, and that we needed to be taken somewhere? He never asked us any questions about mother at all." Bain sat back as memories began to play in his head and things began piecing together.

"Kreelie, what if they came and took her again? What am I supposed to do?" Bain said, standing and pacing the floor.

"We'll figure it out, Bain. We have resources at academy we can use to search. I'll help you look day and night if you want?"

"Thanks, Kreelie. I don't know what I'd do without my best friend to talk to."

Kreelie grinned broadly. "That's what a best friend is for, man."

"I'll be sixteen in a couple of months and eligible to graduate academy. When I do, I'm going to use everything I can to find my mom again. And, to get my siblings away from my grandfather. In the meantime, I'm going to search grandfather's office, daily if I can, for any clues as to his participation."

"If you need me to be a lookout or cause a distraction while you look, I'd be glad to help. Besides, it will give me practice and experience for that drama academy you keep telling me I need to enter," Kreelie grinned.

"Thanks, Kreelie. Just give me a few days to study the schedules of everyone in the house, then we can make a plan of attack. We have to be extra careful, because if grandfather suspects that I know anything, I'm not sure what he'll do. I used to think I knew him. Now remember, you *have to promise* that you won't tell a soul. I mean it, Kreelie. Not even my siblings."

Kreelie stood at attention and saluted Bain in an animated manner, "Sir, you have my word, Sir," and then he grinned again.

Kreelie was a good guy and didn't divulge secrets on purpose, but he was a talker and sometimes spoke before thinking about what he was saying. Bain would tell Seadon and Wynne, just as soon as he thought that it was okay to do so. He really wanted to wait until he found his mother again before he revealed to them that she was alive. The less people who knew right now the better. He just sincerely hoped that trusting Kreelie with such a secret would prove beneficial. He had managed to keep Bain's secret about the uplink hunt for his mother that he had been doing for the last year or so, surely he could manage a few months more with this new secret.

Chapter 12

The Talks

Finn sat at the sidewalk table outside the restaurant waiting for whoever contacted him to show up. He glanced around at the people passing by on the crowded walkways when he noticed a very attractive, dark-haired woman, her hair pulled back into a low bun. She was dressed in a very nice button-down dress shirt, straight-line, knee-length skirt, and black open toe heels, coming straight for him. She walked up to his table, leaned over, and kissed him on the cheek.

"Hello, darling, so sorry I'm late," she said, sitting at the table like they had known each other forever. Finn studied her for just a second. The black of her hair made the deep blue of her eyes pop.

Finn decided to play along, realizing this woman must be the contact who he was to meet with. He cleared his throat, sat up taller, and replied.

"Not a problem, sweetheart, I'd wait for you all day," he said, really smiling at her, as he took her hand and brushed a kiss across the top of her knuckles. He noticed the look of surprise briefly pass across her features.

"Did you order for me yet?" she asked, now teasing him just slightly as the waiter approached their table.

"No, I wasn't sure what you would be in the mood for today," he answered, smiling at the waiter as he handed them the menu. They both ordered quickly, then waited for the waiter to set the water glasses down before starting the conversation.

"My Uncle who lives in Loradin wants us to come for a visit tomorrow. Do you think that would be possible?" she asked watching him with all seriousness now.

"I don't see why we couldn't go. I have nothing pressing to tend to at the moment. What time do you want to leave?" Finn answered.

"How about early in the morning, say six a.m.? He has a project he's been working on that he wishes us to see as soon as possible."

"Six a.m. will be fine. Are you going to pick me up at my place or should we meet at yours?" Finn asked, watching the small smile that formed in the corner of her mouth. She knew he didn't know who she really was, or where she lived.

"What about your place. Besides, I'm much more organized than you are and am likely to be up and about before you even scramble out of bed." She smiled broadly at him, challenging him to reply.

"Perhaps, but I have been up all hours of the night these past few days trying to finish that intra-web search for that special item we discussed. I've barely slept a wink." Finn wondered if she or they, whoever they were, knew about his looking for Harper.

"Yes, I do remember, have you found it yet?"

"No. I've literally searched everywhere I could think of. Do you have any ideas about where to look?"

"Actually, I do," she said with a more serious look on her face. "I think I found that item just last night. My Uncle was a great help in the search, so don't worry about looking anymore. We think we located it for you, and after we leave Uncle's tomorrow, we can go and see about picking it up. That is, if you're free for the whole day?"

"Sweetheart, I have no other plans that are more important than to spend the entire day tomorrow with you."

She smiled broadly; a small bit of color obvious in her cheeks. She continued as the waiter returned with their food orders.

"That's wonderful, darling. It's been simply ages since we've gotten to spend the whole day together completely uninterrupted. I'm very excited for our little trip."

"So am I, sweetheart. More than you can imagine." Finn smiled at her as he forked some food and took a bite. The two of them sat smiling at each other over the meal. They ate making small talk about the food and the weather. When they were finished, the waiter brought the check and the mystery woman said, "My turn to pay, you got the last check. See you in the morning at six, darling," she said, standing and planting another kiss on his cheek before she left.

Finn sat back and watched her go. He had to admit, that little role play game was a lot of fun, especially with a woman as attractive as she was. She had apparently thought it necessary to play the little couples game for a reason. Was he being watched and followed? He was usually better at realizing that he was, but maybe he had been so focused on Harper lately he hadn't noticed. He also had no idea what her name was, who Uncle was, or who they worked for, but he was certain that they were taking a trip to Loradin in the morning to meet him. And whoever they are, they know about Harper and where she was.

Loradin was no easy place to get into, so she must have major clearance with those in charge, or she was going to smuggle him in. Regardless, Finn was ready to get out of Port-Proud. The only reason he was still here was to try and locate Harper. With that taken care of he was clear to go. He took one last drink from his glass, stood, and left the restaurant headed back to his temporary apartment to pack and get ready to leave in the morning. Just in case the woman wasn't the friendly sort after all, he would get in touch with his closest friend and contact here in Port-Proud and inform him of the meeting and what little he garnered from the conversation. He always tried to cover all the bases. He just really hoped she was one of the good guys. It would be a shame if she weren't, he'd really like to get to know her some more.

Finn woke around five a.m. the next morning, walked to the office and checked out of the rental. He returned to the apartment to get everything together before she arrived. He wondered if she were really going to show up, and at six o'clock exactly, he got his answer. There was a knock at the door and when he opened it, she was standing just on the other side.

"Hello, darling. Are you all packed and ready to go? We have a long drive ahead."

"Yes, let me grab my bags," Finn stated. "Oh, by the way, are we taking your Module, or my Voyager," he asked, unsure as to anything at the moment.

"I'm not driving all the way to Loradin on that contraption of yours," she replied as they left the apartment and headed out of the building.

"Contraption? Why does everyone keep calling it a contraption. It happens to be one-of-a-kind. It's destined to be a classic," he defended.

"Classics are another name for expensive, old, pieces of junk," she said, opening the trunk of the luxury Module and letting him place his bags inside.

Finn raised his eyebrows at her comment, which caused her to try and hide the grin trying to form.

"I've been called a classic before. Does that mean you'd consider me a piece of junk?" he asked her as the Module doors opened and they climbed inside. She didn't answer immediately, as they slid into the seats and the engine roared to life.

"I stand corrected," she said with a smirk as she pulled away from the curb and into traffic. Finn grinned broadly at her compliment.

Finn waited for her to explain further now that they were in the safety of the Module and headed out of town.

"Well, Mr. Mobley," she began, "You catch on rather quickly and have a very quick wit. I mistook you for the big buffoon type the first time I saw you."

"I'm not sure how to respond exactly, but I guess I'll just say thank you. You apparently know quite a bit about me, but I am completely in the dark about you, who Uncle is, and where, other than Loradin, it is we are going, and why?"

"I see you understood all my cryptic messages during our conversation yesterday. I'm impressed," she said appreciatively. "My name is Paisley Prince, and I am an agent with the LSS," she noticed the confused look on his face. "Sorry, the Loradin Secret Society. We are special operatives who take care of things that the general citizens of Zanchier -

typically Loradians- don't need to know about, such as the situation with Harper Brinley."

"How do you know of Harper, and if you know about her, why did you wait so long to help her?"

"Well, our organization was only formed seven years ago when the resistance fell apart and was taken over by the thugs known as the Scaithers. They have some very powerful backing and those of us who were honestly trying to help Zanchier and its people went into hiding to regroup and figure out what to do next. We all went through extensive training with the Loradian Government, and this agency was formed. If you hadn't disappeared the night that Harper did, you would have likely been recruited as an agent of the LSS as well. They had collected files on those who were honest and trustworthy. When Harper disappeared from Vassalage three years ago we assumed she died in the bombing of the facility. It wasn't until the Fenore Winterfest event that we had any clue she was still alive. The only problem was that we weren't the only ones who found out. Commander Raif Martray was once one of the higher up leaders of the resistance, but quickly turned bad and took up with other like-minded people forming the group known as the Scaithers."

"Yes, I know of Martray. I served under him when the resistance started. I have to say though, that your LSS didn't do such a thorough job on their files if they thought I was the honest and trustworthy type back then. I used to be an assassin for whoever paid enough."

"Yes, we know, but that was back before the resistance formed. We know everything about your past, Mr. Mobley. Including what Martray ordered to be done with your family," she said, looking at him with understanding.

"You mean to tell me that Commander Raif Martray is the man responsible for having my family murdered?" Finn fumed.

"I'm so sorry, I thought you knew that already," she stammered a little, feeling his mood shift to one of anger.

"No, I didn't. But now that you say it, it makes perfect sense. He was the one who tried to talk me into joining the resistance against the corrupt government. But I told him I was happy with my life the way it was. I wasn't interested in resisting the government. They were making me a very rich man. A week later, my home was raided, me and my family taken into custody under the pretense that it was the corrupt Zanchieth government doing so. Then they murdered my wife and children in front of me. They then said that I had gotten what I deserved and had thrown me into the streets a broken man. Martray was the one who supposedly found me, took me in, and talked me into getting even with the people who did this to me. I thought it was someone else this whole time and it had been Martray all along, pulling on his little puppet strings."

"Mr. Mobley…"

"You can call me Finn," he grinned a little, even if it was a forced one. "Besides, sweetheart, I think we've moved past the whole formal thing don't you?"

She laughed at his remark, "I suppose you're right, darling," she replied with a twinkle in her eye. "Sorry for springing that on you, but you handled it very well. Your quick wit and charm took me utterly by surprise. You even managed to make me blush just a tad."

"Yes, I noticed that." He grinned honestly this time. "Why the role play anyway? Were we, or I, being watched by someone?"

"I couldn't be certain, but since they so quickly made Harper, we couldn't take any chances."

"How did you know that I had been involved with Harper?"

"We've been watching the Fenore estate for some-time now. We have reason to believe that Derek Fenore is involved with the crooked side of the Zanchieth government. We had operatives stationed at the Winterfest event watching certain people suspected of Scaither sympathy when we realized who she was. It was such a break for our agency. She is a very important woman. Anyway, we saw her and you communicating slightly at the party, then had you followed and have been monitoring your activities ever since. We noticed you were scanning the intra-web with a Palm-Cast looking for Harper. I'm also interested where you got such a device?"

"I had no idea I was being watched by your agency. I'm usually much better at tracking such things. And, I have a lot of old contacts that help me out when I need it."

"Well, don't feel bad. We trained long and hard to learn not to be seen if we didn't want to be."

"So, is Uncle the LSS?"

"Yes, sort of. I'll introduce you to the man we call Uncle later. You do catch on quickly," she said appreciatively.

"I'm not such a buffoon after all, then?" he grinned.

"No, not at all," she smiled. "In fact, I'd say you are quite intelligent and would make a great asset to the LSS as an agent."

"I don't know about all of that, but I'll keep it in mind. I'm not sure what I'm going to end up doing now that Harper seems to have the good guys on her side. I've spent the last five years helping her survive, learn to fight, and helping to find her family. After all of this is over, I'm going to have to find a new life."

"Well, just remember, we at the LSS would certainly consider your joining us a bonus."

"Just the LSS?" Finn pressed her.

She smiled at his question, "I have to say that I personally would enjoy having you around as well."

Finn grinned from ear to ear right along with Paisley. The two made small talk for the next four hours as they drove along the Everly Lake coastline and through the Carpasian Mountains to the southern side of Zanchier.

Finn sat and took in the wild beauty of the countryside while Paisley masterfully steered the Module along the winding roads. He had truly never been to this side of Zanchier before. With Loradin being so hard to gain entry into, he had no reason to. Loradin was like a separate country all together with some serious border-patrol. As they drew nearer to the city, Finn could see the tall spires of the glistening buildings shining in the noon day sun. The city of Loradin sat on an island in Everly Lake, which acted like a giant moat, surrounding, and protecting the city from would-be invaders. As they grew closer, Finn could see a port on the north-eastern side of the city where many boats docked. He could also see a check-in station which each boat that wished to moor up to the city's port had to pass through. On the eastern shore of the city was a beautifully crafted flat bridge which they had to cross in order to enter the city gates. Finn noticed that even the small villages, such as Praxtingen, that sat on the land side of Loradin seemed to be flourishing as well. Very contradictory to the suffering lower classes of Bakrashan and Carpasmere. Even the citizens of those classes who worked inside the larger cities weren't as well off as the same class of citizens living here near Loradin. What did the Loradians know about living that the rest of Zanchier did not?

Passing over the bridge, Finn noticed all the Modules pulling into a checkpoint before passing through the gates. He also noticed Paisley push a button on the roof of her Module and an inside-lane magically appeared on the road to their left, allowing only her to bypass the checkpoint. Their Module was the only vehicle traveling the clear, glass-like lower lane through the city gates.

Finn looked out the window and down below the Module. His stomach turned ever so slightly at the large expanse of water far beneath them. It appeared as though their Module was flying. Finn sat back against his seat, taking a deep breath, and sighing heavily.

Paisley smiled broadly at the look of nausea that seemed to overtake the large, muscular, man sitting beside her.

"Are you afraid of heights?" she asked amused.

"Not normally," he replied straight-faced. "Only when it looks like there's no road beneath me."

"You'll get used to it," she reassured him with a grin.

They were through the gates and inside the city before Finn knew it. Loradin was truly magical looking. He had never seen anything that compared. Martanzia, Port-Proud, and Everly-Sound were places that he had considered very beautiful to see, but none of them could compare to the fantastic architecture, layout, and overall beauty of Loradin. No wonder this place was so hard to get into.

Paisley pulled the Module to a stop at what appeared to be a restaurant. "Why don't we grab some lunch before getting down to business. It's going to be a long day and there's no point in going in on an empty stomach."

"Sounds good to me," Finn agreed as he followed her inside the establishment, "Long day, huh?" Finn questioned.

"Yes. Not to mention the very soon attempt at retrieving Harper Brinley," she said, her demeanor suddenly turning very serious. Finn wondered if he really knew what he was getting himself into. He was about to find out, one way or the other.

Chapter 13

The Resistance

Harper sat at the large table, tools in hand, slaving over the large weapon that she was being forced to help build. She wasn't the only scientist that had been captured and forced to work for the government or the Scaithers. She was really unsure who her captors were. She looked around the room at the others there, about ten people in all in this particular room. *What were their stories?* she wondered. *Who were they being kept from, or who had been killed or threatened with death to make them cooperate?*

Harper used to grow angry at this question, but with her recapture, she just wanted to finish their stupid weapon and get out of Vassalage as quickly as possible. If they didn't release her then, the sooner her death the better. She was tired of running, and she knew she would never be able to go back to her old life. Her children seemed happy and well-adjusted with her parents.

Harper wondered if her parents and children were all right? She hoped that her reappearance into society hadn't endangered them in any way. She had asked Martray about them, and he told her that they were fine and would remain so as long as she cooperated. But if she tried to escape again, he wouldn't be so kind. Not only would he hurt Harper, but her family as well. So, she had been cooperating like she never had before. She didn't know whether he was telling her the truth or not, but she had no choice but to believe him. If, however, she did get out of Vassalage, and any of her family had been harmed, then she would return and kill Martray with her own two hands. She made sure he knew it too. The day she had asked about them, and he assured her they were fine, she told him as much. The look on his face was one of amusement. She remembered what he had said to her.

"Well, now, Harper. I don't remember you being so tough before. Spirited yes, but threatening, you weren't. What happened to you after your escape to turn you into the vigilante type?"

"You did, Martray. You and your outlaw band of Scaithers and the terror that you lay across the lands of Zanchier," she had replied.

"Well, I see my reputation proceeds itself, even to the furthest reaches of Zanchier," he cockily and proudly stated.

"It wasn't a compliment," she stated flatly.

"I know. But I see it as one regardless. If people fear me, then all the better. I want them to, and they should. You see, Harper, fear is a great motivator. People will do virtually anything out of fear. Whether it be for themselves or for their loved ones. Hatred also works if used in the right manner. I've motivated many a man based on the hatred that I created in them myself. I've learned to manipulate and twist the element of human emotion to garner anything that I wish, no matter how large or how small the conquest is. It's all very…stimulating," he bragged with such an air of arrogance that Harper could have killed him right then if she had a weapon to do so.

"You're a sick man, Martray," she had stated.

He walked up to her, grabbed her face with his hand and leaned in almost touching her nose with his, "Perhaps, Harper, but I am a man with a mission which makes me very dangerous indeed. If you're not careful, I might just take an interest in you. And don't forget, I always get what I want, so you better be very careful what you say to me or how you treat me. You see, I have this nagging desire to get even when people wrong me, and I just can't quench that thirst until I fulfill it," he said, smiling sleazily at her before he slowly let her go and backed away.

"I'll die first," she said, knowing full well what his threat insinuated.

"That can be arranged," he said growing agitated.

"You won't kill me until I've finished your weapon. You need me too much or it would have been completed years ago. So, unless you want to postpone having it finished indefinitely, you'll stay as far from me and my family as you can get. And I want proof, visual proof that every one of my children and my parents are safe."

He sat and looked at her for several seconds before answering.

"All right, Harper. I can tell you mean what you say and so I'll oblige your request, for now. But don't push your luck, Brinley," he said, turning away from her as he instructed the guards to return her to her cell. "Oh, one more thing, Harper. Are you certain you wish to barter for the lives of your parents as well? You really don't know them as well as you think you do, you know," he said, turning to her again to watch the seed of doubt that he had planted take root and begin to crawl through the recesses of her mind. He smiled that sleazy smile once again as the guard pulled her from his office.

Harper snapped back to reality when she burnt her fingers with the soldering gun. She hadn't realized that she had zoned out. She sucked the offending finger hoping to stop some of the burning. She stood up and walked to the sink to run cold water over the burning skin as the comment about her parents returned to her mind.

What did he mean by her not knowing her parents very well, or that she shouldn't concern herself with worrying about them? He hadn't said those words exactly, but she knew what he had meant, sort of. What she didn't know was why he had said that. Did he know something about her parents that she didn't? Her father had always had business deals that neither she, nor her mother, knew anything about. Surely her father wasn't involved with people like the Scaithers, or Martray? Harper did recall once when she was around twelve years old, she had seen Vonder Mortruff leaving her father's office late one night. He was one of the most underhanded and dangerous men in Martanzia. She remembered seeing him sitting at her father's table at the Winterfest event last week as well. She hadn't thought about that until now, and she wondered what sort of dealings her father could have with a man like Mortruff?

Harper shook the thoughts from her mind, dried off her hand, added a bandage, and returned to her spot at the table to continue working. Perhaps concentrating on the weapon would allow all the thoughts flying through her mind to disappear for a while.

After lunch Paisley took Finn to the tallest building that he had ever seen. It was by far the tallest one in Loradin. She pulled the Module into a parking garage beneath the building, and the two of them took an elevator to the second highest floor. When Finn stepped off the elevator, he was stunned by the view. The entire wall was nothing but glass, and it afforded a spectacular, one-hundred-and-eighty-degree view of the city. He could also see the harbor and docks with the check-in station off in the distance. As they walked the curving hallway, the scenery outside the windows changed as different areas of the city below came into view.

"Whew…," Finn whistled lowly to himself.

"Pretty spectacular view isn't it?" Paisley said, in reply to his reaction.

"Yeah, pretty unbelievable. I've never been this high up before."

As they walked a few more steps, Paisley opened a door in the interior wall, and he followed her inside. Standing behind a large steel and glass desk was a man close in age to Finn. The man looked up as Paisley and Finn entered.

"Finn Mobley, this is Aaric Brinley, also known as Uncle to all of us who are agents here."

"Mr. Mobley, nice to meet you," Aaric said, extending his hand to Finn.

"Brinley," Finn said, shaking the man's hand, "any relation to Harper Brinley?"

"Yes. She happens to be my daughter-in-law," the man said through a thin, worried smile.

"And you're just now searching for her why?" Finn asked a bit perturbed that it had taken them this long to find her.

"I'm certain Paisley briefed you on all of this already," Aaric said, curiously.

"Yeah, she did. But I've seen what Harper has been through over the last five years. Why did you let her stay in Vassalage for two years? Why didn't you try and get her out then?"

"We did. Through the resistance that you yourself were a part of. Only then we didn't realize that there were traitors running the missions."

"Paisley said your agency has been running for seven years. That's two years before Harper was even taken. How did they take her to begin with if you were already a working agency?"

"We were just starting out at that time and our manpower was limited I'm afraid. That's why we couldn't stop them from taking Wilkins either."

Finn started at the mention of Aaric's son Wilkins.

"Sorry, I didn't think about what I was saying."

"Not to worry, I understand your line of questioning. Now, back to the mission at Vassalage five years ago. We sent people in to free the scientists imprisoned there, but Martray had ordered a killing spree. We found the charred remains of a woman in Harper's cell, who fit her size and shape. We assumed that Harper was either killed by a weapon, or during the bombing of the building. We truly had no idea that she had escaped until last week when she appeared out of nowhere after three long years. Not to mention that she looked nothing like her old self. Brilliant work by the way. I'd like to know who helped with her transformation. I could use someone like that on our team here."

"I'll get your number to her," Finn stated.

"I suppose you're wondering why you're here, Mr. Mobley," Aaric said, motioning for Finn to have a seat, then sitting himself.

Finn didn't answer, only took the seat as offered.

"We need your help to get Harper out of Vassalage and then to destroy the building and all the plans for the weapon that they are trying to assemble."

"Why me? It seems to me that you have all the equipment and people you could ever need right here."

"We are very well staffed and provided for by the governing members of Loradin, but you have already been inside once and may know exactly where they are keeping her. And she obviously trusts you."

"If you can get Harper out of that place, I'm in. I just need one thing," Finn said with a smirk.

"Whatever you need Mr. Mobley, we'll do whatever we can to get it for you," Aaric stated.

"My Voyager. We had to leave it back in Port-Proud."

Paisley stepped forward and interjected, "That's already been taken care of Finn. Your Voyager will be at your new residence when we arrive there later. I saw to the shipping myself."

Finn smiled at her, "Thanks for that."

"Of course," she said, all business like.

"Now, Mr. Mobley, let's get you settled into your new living quarters and we will debrief you at seven tomorrow morning."

Aaric turned to Paisley, "Get his paperwork completed this evening and make sure his security clearances are all taken care of. Oh, and get him a Mod will you?"

"I don't need a Module, I have my Voyager," Finn replied.

"No offense, Mr. Mobley, but your Voyager, as you call it, is no match for our newer mods."

"Well, if you've got the place and equipment, then I can upgrade it to make it even better."

Aaric sighed, "Well if you insist on a make-over, then don't worry, I'll have our technicians start work on it within the hour." He pushed a button on his desk and spoke into the air. "Kinley, I need a transport over to Mr. Mobley's place and the package delivered there earlier to be taken to the lab for an overhaul."

"Right away, Uncle," came a female voice across the line.

"I can do the work myself, I prefer it actually," Finn protested.

"No time for that Mr. Mobley. You have too much training and paperwork to see to. Besides the mission to rescue Harper will happen tomorrow evening and your Voyager will need to be operational."

"You people don't waste any time do you?" Finn asked, astounded.

"Time is of the utmost importance, Mr. Mobley. We need to get Harper out of Vassalage before the weapon can be completed. If they finish it, it could mean ruin and destruction for everyone who lives in Zanchier."

"What exactly is this weapon she's supposed to be able to build anyway? She never really understood what it was for."

"That's because Harper's expertise is the firing mechanism. There are many other scientists that are being held as well, all of whom we are planning on freeing. Each group has a unique talent or gift in their field of study. According to our spy on the inside, there are seven steps to the making of the weapon. Harper and the other nine scientists are step seven. If they manage to complete the firing mechanism, then Martray will have them all to assemble the weapon. If that happens, our world as we know it will no longer exist. The weapon is like a matter dissolver. With a weapon like that, Martray would be able to erase anyone and anything from existence with the push of a button."

"That doesn't sound good at all. He could wipe out whoever he wanted."

"Not only people, but places, buildings, vegetation. Any matter at all, Mobley. Creation itself will be at the mercy of people like Martray. He isn't the only one seeking such weapons either. There are many people in government, the Zanchieths, Martans, and yes even some Loradians, who would pay dearly for it. Can you imagine the destruction that would take place in a matter of days if people got their hands on such a weapon? The effects would be devastating and unrepairable. So yes, haste is of the utmost importance."

"What about Harper's family? What happens to them?" Finn asked, concerned where all this could be going.

"We have measures in place to bring her children here to Loradin at the time she's rescued."

"And her parents? I don't think those kids would leave without them. Especially Harper's mother Gracelynn. Adda, the youngest has only ever known Derek and Gracleynn Fenore as parents."

"We've made…arrangements for them as well, should the need arise."

"Arrangements? That doesn't sound too reassuring."

"Derek Fenore has been under investigation and surveillance for some time now. He may even be one of the bidders who are requesting a weapon. Not to mention that we think he was the one who turned Harper over to Martray. We can't be certain, but we aren't willing to risk our agents to protect him."

"Why would he do that to his own daughter?"

"We don't know, but that is one of the reasons that he is being watched very closely."

"Okay, I get leaving Derek Fenore, but what about Gracelynn? I'm pretty certain, just from talking to her that she has no idea about any of this," Finn said.

"We will do what we can. But Harper and the children are our first priority above all else, simply because of Harper's importance and the fact that they are my grandchildren as well, my wife and I have been without seeing them for far too long."

"Understood," Finn said standing. "Where do I start?"

Chapter 14

The Weapon

"All right, Finn, here is your new home," Paisley said, unlocking the door and ushering him inside.

Finn looked over his new place as part of the LSS. He had to say, they certainly took care of their agents. The apartment was very nice, and the view from the wall of windows and glass doors which led out to a balcony off the living area, lent a spectacular view of the city and the harbor, which looked to be about a mile away. It wasn't as tall as the skyscraper that the LSS was located in, but Finn preferred shorter buildings anyway.

"Nice place."

"Yes, well, there are other benefits to being part of the LSS. Of course, the dangers of what we do are far greater than any other career, so they make sure that when we are home, we are taken care of well. Not to mention the Rhedon is nice. All living expenses paid, plus a hefty salary. But the most satisfying part of the work is catching the criminals and helping the people of Zanchier."

"You seem pretty passionate about your work," Finn said.

"Yes, I am, when you're born into the Bakrisian class and have no hope at a better life, and when someone gives you the opportunity, you're grateful for it," she stated looking at him.

"I understand that. That's the reason I turned to assassination. I was Carpasian but not from the Loradian boundaries. I hail from Carpasmere, one of the poorest in the regions. When I was fourteen, I moved into Bakrashan. I was young, foolish, and full of myself. I had mad skills with weapons and easily got mixed up with the wrong sort. I was compensated well for those skills, took to assassination, and here I am."

"Yes, but you turned from your old life, and now you serve the people."

"Yes, but it cost me everything I held dear."

"I know of your pain, Finn," she said placing her hand on his arm. "But there is One who can ease that pain."

"He has eased it already, but it isn't something that I will completely get over or ever forget. My family suffered the cruelest of fates because of the life choices that I made early on. The path that I chose was one of Rhedon, glory, and hatred. When I tried to leave it all behind, they paid the price."

"So have you," she offered.

"Yes, but at least I'm still alive. Sometimes I wish I weren't. The haunting visions are so strong, but I know I was left here for a reason. And I think what I'm doing right now, helping Harper, is where I'm supposed to be."

Paisley smiled at Finn, "All right, well then, let's get you settled and on the way to the office. We'll stop in and have a look at the progress they are making with your Voyager. I overheard the buzz in the office about the excitement the Techs have about enhancing that thing. We may have more of them to look forward to in the future."

"It is a blast to drive," he smiled.

The two of them left Finn's large flat and headed back to the LSS to the lab which was tech central. As they walked through the part-laden area, Finn noticed tables filled with all manner of equipment, corners stacked with new developments, and people milling about working on all sorts of things. People stopped moving, staring at him a bit as they walked through the room. In the back, in a large area, sat his Voyager, somewhat stripped down, but with a few new shiny parts beginning to be added back on. There were two younger men and one very young woman who were talking excitedly about what should be done or what would be added next.

Paisley stopped in front of them and cleared her throat to get their attention. Everyone stopped their chatting and looked at her.

"Paisley," they yelled almost in unison, "thanks for this thing," they said excitedly as they pointed to the Voyager, "it's been a blast to work on. Whoever came up with this design was a genius, it just needs a bit of tweaking."

Paisley smiled and waved her hand in Finn's direction. "Let me then introduce you to the genius himself. This is Finn Mobley." She then turned to Finn, "Finn, this is Cranston, Winnie, and Maubry."

Maubry quickly grabbed Finn's outstretched hand with both of his, shaking it fiercely, "So nice to meet you Mr. Mobley. Your contraption, the Voyager as you call it, is like nothing we've ever seen before. It's been such a privilege to play with it and see how to improve it."

"Well, Maubry, I'm glad you're enjoying working on my *contraption*," Finn said, a little perturbed that everyone called it that, "But just be sure you know what you're doing. It took me a while to get it just right, and she's a fine piece of machinery if I do say so myself."

"Oh, yes sir, Mr. Mobley," Maubry said, genuinely grinning at Finn, "I do see that you've done a nice job of putting it together, but I must say that we do know what we are doing, and I promise to have it back to you much better by tomorrow morning. You'll see," the excited little man finished saying.

"Yes, well, let's hope so. At least maybe have it put back together so that I can use it. It's my only mode of transport," Finn said, a bit irritated as he scanned the parts and pieces of his precious Voyager that were lying about.

"Most certainly, Sir. You can rest easily knowing that she is in good hands."

Finn still wasn't convinced, but the other two known as Cranston and Winnie confirmed Maubry's confidence with an enthusiastic shake of their heads.

Paisley could see the look of concern on Finn's face. "Don't worry, Finn. Your Voyager is in excellent hands. Those three are the best in their field."

She smiled at the concerned look on Finn's tortured face as he glanced back at the jumbled mess of parts that was once his one-of-a-kind Voyager.

"Oh, Finn, we have another surprise for you," she stated with a smile.

"I'm not sure I can take any more surprises like the last one."

Paisley laughed at his statement as they rounded the corner and entered another room. There, at some tables with a whole lot of interesting-looking equipment, was Kamsten Whitsler.

"Kam?" Finn asked, "What are you doing here?"

"I was convinced to join the LSS. They gave me my own lab where I get to create whatever invention I want. At their expense! Plus, their paying me big bucks, I have an apartment, and a Module," she said with a wide-eyed, shocked grin.

Finn looked at Paisley, "You people certainly work quickly," he said.

"Yes, we do," she said with a cocky smirk.

Kamsten whispered to Finn, "They said they were the good guys. Are they?"

"Not sure myself yet, Kam. But as soon as I have it figured out, I'll let you know."

Kamsten shook her head at his reply and went back to work developing her next big invention called image enhancers. Devices that would allow someone to temporarily change their appearance with cloaking-type technology.

Finn and Paisley then went into debriefing with the other agents who were to accompany them on the mission to retrieve Harper and to free the other scientists. Finn only hoped that these people were on the level. The last attempt like this was a set up and ended badly for a lot of people. But since Harper was directly related to the man in charge, surely they were being truthful.

There was to be a team of about twenty people who would be entering Vassalage on this mission. Each group of two would have a different objective. Finn and one other agent known simply as Will, would see to freeing Harper. Finn was a little bummed about his partner. He had hoped that he would be storming Vassalage with Paisley. He couldn't wait to see her in action.

After the meeting and getting their orders for the mission, Paisley ordered food to be dropped to Finn at his apartment and took him home. Finn bid her goodnight, entered his apartment just before his dinner was delivered, ate, showered, and slid into bed. He was exhausted by the day's events and everything he saw, heard, and learned today. In the morning, they would leave for the backside of the Carpasian Mountains where the Scaither's secret prison and laboratory was located. They would wait until dark, which came early with the winter season still upon them. Then they would set their plan in motion. They would have exactly fifteen minutes in which to accomplish their missions or they would all die in the bombing of the facility. The main objective was to destroy the weapon that was being created. Everyone knew the risks, and everyone was willing to pay the ultimate price for the future of Zanchier.

Finn woke early, feeling rested from the hard sleep the night before. Paisley appeared just after seven a.m. to collect him. They were all to meet at headquarters by eight to get ready to head out by ten. Apparently, they were to take a transport to the Loradin Airship Field. Finn had never flown before and didn't even know that the technology to do so already existed. He wondered how this was all going to work since they were supposed to transport several mods and his Voyager. That is, if Maubry and his tech crew had gotten it finished.

Paisley wanted to collect him early enough to swing by the technical lab so he could see the upgrades they had made to the Voyager.

Finn followed Paisley through the building once again, nervous to see his Voyager, hoping that it wasn't still in pieces. Much to his surprise the Voyager was complete, and he hardly recognized it. The upgrades they had made to it made it sleek, shiny, and sexy looking.

"Whew..." Finn whistled long and slow. "Maubry, Winnie, Cranston, I am totally shocked at what you three accomplished in what, sixteen hours? I can't believe that it's the same machine."

"So, you're pleased with the upgrades?" Maubry asked anxiously.

"Well, it looks the part, but what does it sound like?" Finn asked, hoping it started because he really wanted to take it for a spin.

"Wonderful. It purrs like a newborn Pagorinx. Not that I've actually seen a newborn Pagorinx up close, or ever seen a Pagorinx in person for that matter," Maubry said, chattering as usual.

"May I?" Finn asked, pointing at his Voyager.

"Certainly, Mr. Mobley. It is, after all, yours."

Finn walked over to the machine, running his hand down the smooth, shiny, highly polished metal. He straddled the seat, turned the igniter, and pushed the button on the handles. The Voyager roared to life and truly did purr like a Pagorinx. He remembered the first encounter with the cub that was hunting him, and the purring noise it made while waiting to pounce on him.

"Maubry, you've outdone yourselves," Finn said appreciatively.

"I'm glad you're happy but there are many upgrades to the machine. We've taken the liberty of drawing up the schematics and all the added weapons features. May I suggest you spend the time on the airship transport today studying your new Voyager before pushing any of the extra buttons?" Maubry said, a bit nervously.

"Sure thing, Maubry. I can take a hint. So, do I just ride it out of here now?"

"No. We'll have it delivered to the airfield and it will be loaded on board the airship by the time you all arrive later."

"Well, all right then. I'm itching to ride her, but I'll take your advice and read up on it first."

Finn and Paisley left to meet with Uncle and the other agents to get all the tech devices they would need for the mission. They each were given wrist communicators to be able to talk with each other, weapons to strap anywhere they chose, camouflage as black as night so as not to be seen, and night vision glasses so that they could approach the facility without using their Mod lights.

Finn was impressed by the organization of this group. But what really impressed him was seeing the massive airship in which they were to board and float high above Zanchier.

Paisley had tried to explain some about it before they arrived but what lay before Finn was astonishing. He didn't understand how they could get something that large off the ground and actually float through the sky with it. The top of the airship was apparently where the light-weight but sturdy canvas material was filled with the gas that would make the ship rise. The material was lightly held in place by a cabling system that wrapped across the material in several different directions and anchored to the split-level passenger area beneath it. As they walked on board, Paisley gave him a tour of the airship before they had to leave.

The top of the passenger car, from about waist high, was surrounded by reinforced, shatterproof, thick glass windows, and there were chairs comfortably scattered throughout the front half. The back half had a kitchen, infirmary, and about ten separate sleeping quarters. The bottom floor of the airship was surrounded by metal. That was where Finn could see the mods being loaded with only a few to go. A large ramp style door lay down from the back of the airship and the mods were driven inside. The front half of the bottom of the ship also had a few large, glass windows where there were more sleeping quarters and a small sitting area. In the very front of this small sitting area was a door leading to the control room and wheelhouse for the ship. The whole front of the small room was all glass on three sides, giving the pilot complete visibility. Paisley told him that the airship had at least twenty sleeping quarters in all. The crew used the bottom front half of the airships first three rooms. The captain had his own quarters, the two mates shared a room, and the four other crew members shared one of the other sleeping quarters. After the quick tour they walked topside, Paisley leaving him to tend to some necessary business.

Finn took a seat with the rest of the team and pulled out his manual to learn about his old friend. He hoped he would be able to concentrate on the manual and not spend all of his time on the flight looking out of the massive windows which showed the beauty of Zanchier from every angle.

Harper and the other nine scientists had been working all day on the weapon and tried to stall the finishing of it for as long as they could, but they had already been stalling for the last two days. Martray knew they were close and was growing impatient. Harper looked at the final piece of the puzzle and hoped that it just wouldn't work, but she doubted that would happen. The weapon was rather large and would have to be mounted on a base to move it around or operate it. She figured that Martray already had that made. So, if it worked it could be used immediately.

"Go ahead, Harper, just install the coupling and be done with it. We can't keep stalling any longer, you know that. All we can do is hope that something goes wrong, and it doesn't work," one of the other scientists told her, as they all watched.

Martray had been observing the group for the last hour and knew something was going on because they didn't all usually gather in one spot.

"They've finished it," he said, a wicked smile breaking out across his face. He quickly entered the room and walked up behind Harper. "Well, Harper, is it done?"

Harper sighed heavily, "We believe so."

"What does that mean exactly?" Martray questioned.

"We don't know if it will actually work, Martray. It is only theory that it will even power on."

"Well, for all of your sakes, it had better do something. I've waited for five years for this to be finished. Guards," he barked, "load the weapon onto the base and let's wheel it outside. I want a demonstration. Oh, and bring them all along. I want them to witness the fruits of their labor." Martray smiled.

The guards returned within ten minutes with about eight other guards to heft the large gun onto the base. It took all they could give to move the thing into position. They hoped that the base would actually move now that the weapon had been loaded upon it. It was so heavy that it took about four of the guards and a total of twenty minutes to push it through the facility and outside the building.

It was early evening, just before dark when Martray pointed the weapon at a small range of hills located far across the valley from the mountain where Vassalage sat. He turned on the weapon and it hummed to life, with a series of clicks, power surges, and crackles of electricity. Martray beamed as he looked excitedly at the weapon before him.

"This will be a momentous occasion for the resistance," Martray laughed, knowing the resistance was no longer what it had started out as. "Harper, would you like to do the honors on your baby here?" he grinned at her.

Harper glowered at him. He knew she wanted nothing to do with the weapon, and she secretly hoped that it wouldn't work, or exploded upon use, taking Martray down with the machine.

"No?" he acted surprised. "Would any of the rest of you like to push the button first?" he asked, tormenting them with the fact that they had actually created this thing. They feared what it would do and on what scale. They all stood there, shaking their heads no, while Martray laughed at them.

"Well, then, it appears that the honors are all mine."

Martray aimed the beam at the small grouping of hills about five miles across the valley that lay between them. He flipped up a clear, protective, glass cover, and pushed the button. The weapon hummed louder, and the sound escalated as it gathered the needed energy to fire. In a matter of about ten seconds, the weapon let loose of a blast of energized light which streaked across the five-mile distance in a matter of only seconds and obliterated the small range of hills. They were completely gone. They all stood there gaping at the destruction. As they watched, where the hills once stood, appeared to be a series of small tornadic winds that began to grow in intensity, churning constantly. The small tornadoes seemed to be contained to the area where the hills once sat. The only thing left was the constantly circulating dirt and sand, and around six tornadoes ranging in size.

Martray laughed out loud, excited over the results as the rest of the scientists and even some of the guards were terrified over what they had just witnessed. They all prayed that the hills which no longer existed had not been populated by any of the citizens of Zanchier.

Good Heavens! Harper thought, *this is madness! I can't let this weapon do any more damage.*

Finn and the others sped along the long, dark, twisting mountain highway headed toward Vassalage on the outskirts of Bakrashan and Carpasmere. The facility was well hidden in the dense mountainous forest that surrounded it. It had been relocated since the last time it had been attacked and nearly burnt to the ground. At that time, it had been a government run prison. When last attacked by the resistance, otherwise known as his organization, the Scaithers, Commander Raif Martray decided to move the facility to a more secure location.

Finn's Voyager ran and rode like a dream, and he couldn't wait to try out the new features that the manual boasted that was now installed. As the line of cars, hidden by the darkness of the moonless night streaked quickly along the road, Finn noticed a glow coming from the direction of the facility off in the distance. They were only a few miles from the facility now and he wondered what it could be. Within a matter of seconds, he saw and heard a blast that emanated from the glow and streaked across the valley below the mountain road. A loud explosion erupted in the nearby hills. All the teams quickly slammed on the brakes and stepped out of their mods as they looked at the now gaping hole in the hillside. As they watched the dust clearing it began to swirl and turn, sucking the air all around them into the vortexes of spinning air, sand, dirt, and whatever else was left standing after the blast had finished its work.

"What in heavens name was that?" Finn exclaimed out loud. The other agents all could hear him through their communicators and replied in kind.

"I have no idea, but I think it may have to do with the weapon Martray wanted built," Paisley stated, stunned as they watched the storm building, and the vortexes that were forming and pulling the air and other loose debris into the spinning, darkening, shapes.

"Then we better get a move on and stop that maniac before there's nothing left of Zanchier," Finn stated, taking off as fast as he could, followed by the team of six transport mods filled with nineteen other agents. All now desperate to stop Commander Raif Martray at any cost.

Chapter 15

The Breakout

Harper decided that it was time to use the skills in which she had trained for over the last three years. She elbowed the guard next to her in the stomach, and then punched him in the face, taking his weapon in the process. She then shot two others before they even knew what was happening.

Martray, realizing what was going on, yelled at Harper.

"No! Harper stop!" he ordered, but the guards were at a disadvantage and he was without his gun this evening. He ran inside the facility as an all-out fight began between the scientists and the remaining other five guards. A few of the scientists were mortally wounded and a few others sustained injuries as they overtook the guards, killing them all. Martray watched from inside the facility as Harper turned off the weapon and ripped some of the internal wires out to disable the machine. She then turned her gun on it and began firing to disable it even more.

Martray screamed in anger as he watched her begin destroying the machine, and he was unable to stop her.

"Harper stop firing at that thing. It's liable to explode!" one of the others yelled to her.

"I hope it does! I can't allow it to be used again!" she said, continuing to fire. Everyone began running for cover and for their lives as they realized there was no one to stop them now.

Harper backed away from the weapon as she continued firing upon it, filling it with as many holes as she could manage. It began to spark and sizzle as flames began to shoot out of the weapon in several spots. Harper had just fired the last remaining rounds of the gun when smoke began to roil up and electrical parts began to pop and sizzle. Harper threw down the gun, turned, and began to run when the weapon exploded, sending pieces of it flying in all directions. She was struck by several pieces of shrapnel. One hitting her in the leg, another in the left shoulder while the blast itself threw her several feet, knocking her out cold as she hit her head on a rock in the ground.

The Vassalage alarm went off as guards scattered to gain control of the situation, and prisoners began to revolt and fight back. The weapons explosion knocked out one of the electrical panels to the building causing the power to go out, and the cell blocks to unlock. People were free, running everywhere and grabbing whatever they could to fight with. Martray retreated to his office, grabbed his handguns and some important papers, went into the hallway, and shot anyone who got in his way, whether it was a guard or a prisoner. He went out the back way of the facility, climbed into his Module, and sped away into the night. He would get even with Harper Brinley if it were the last thing he ever did. If she survived that blast that is! If not, he'd take the issue up with her family. He grinned wickedly as hatred and anger burned through his veins. His Module was pointed toward Port-Proud where he would first meet with Vonder Mortruff about their foiled plans, and then perhaps they would both pay a visit to the Fenore Estate.

As the chaos continued, Finn and the LSS agents all pulled into the facility, discussing a new plan quickly over the communicators. They hadn't planned on an all-out mutiny to be in the works when they arrived. It appeared that someone had taken care of things before they were needed.

Finn and the teams split up to handle finding the scientists, immobilizing any guards they stumbled across. The first thing they did was to see what was blazing behind the building where the blast had come from earlier. The weapon was engulfed in flames and still occasionally spewed sparks and smaller pops and sizzles as it burned away.

Finn figured Harper had to have something to do with it, or it just exploded after use. Perhaps they hadn't figured out how to contain that much power?

"Harper!" Finn began yelling.

"We need to check inside. I don't see why she would be out here," Will stated ready to run into the facility.

"Fine, you check inside if you want. But I know Harper personally, and I bet my life that she had something to do with that thing being destroyed," Finn stated. He began to search the area, dialing up the brightness on the night-vision glasses they had been given and searched the grass around them.

"I know Harper too, and I doubt she would be capable of this," Will stated.

"Look, you might have known Harper before her captivity, but I knew her up until just about a week ago, and I'm telling you, she is very capable of handling herself, especially if it meant saving her family." Finn continued to search the grounds.

Will swallowed hard as he conceded to Finn's knowledge and helped him to search the area around the facility. The light from the burning weapon was still blazing as parts of the ash from the popping began to catch fire to the building as well.

"Paisley," Finn yelled over the comm, "You need to hurry and get everyone out of the building. It's caught fire from the blaze back here."

"Copy that, Finn."

"Paisley, have you seen Harper inside anywhere?"

"No, but one of the scientists that was outside said she was out there and that she was the one who destroyed the weapon."

"I knew it. She must be out here somewhere."

"Finn," Will yelled, "Over here! Harper, are you all right?" Will questioned her, looking over her injuries, noticing the blood on her head, shoulder, and leg.

Finn ran up to her, "She's hurt." Finn pushed past Will, handed him his weapon, picked Harper up, and carried her to one of the Mods with Will close on his heels, taking out any guards that decided they wanted to stop them.

The teams all checked in, stating that all scientists had been freed and whatever guards were alive were in custody. There was a medical team on board the airship just in case anyone was injured during the battle.

"Paisley, can you or someone else ride my Voyager? I've got your Mod. It's urgent, Harper is badly wounded and unresponsive."

"No problem, Finn. We'll see you there."

As the other teams filled the transports to return all the scientists to a safe location until they could be returned home, or put into protective custody, Finn drove the Mod as quickly as possible. Finn prayed to the Creator that Harper would make it. He noticed that Will sat and stared at Harper, a strange look on his face.

"Are you all right, man?" Finn asked, thinking that maybe the man was new or had never seen anyone get hurt.

"I'm fine. Why?"

"You just look a little green around the gills."

"Finn, I don't know exactly what your and Harper's relationship is, but I have to tell you something. My name is Wilkins Brinley. I'm Harper's husband."

Finn was stunned for a moment as he took in the man's stature and appearance. He was a dark-haired man with a full, neatly trimmed mustache and beard. He could see the resemblance to Bain through the eyes now that he knew who he was.

"Our relationship is one of strict friendship. Nothing more. There never has been. All she ever talks about is you." Finn grinned at the man.

The relief that washed over Wilkins was noticeable. "Good. Because you seem like a good man and I didn't want to have to fight you for her," he grinned back.

"You won't have to. Let's just make sure she makes it through this," Finn stated, motioning to the still lifeless form of Harper stretched out in the backseat.

They reached the airship where medics were waiting on them to arrive. They quickly unloaded Harper onto a stretcher, carried her inside, and disappeared into one of the many rooms on board the ship.

Finn and Wilkins sat down in one of the chairs as they waited patiently on news that Harper would be all right. Finn prayed with Wilkins to the Creator to spare her life. After which, Wilkins questioned Finn on Harper's life since he had been taken from his family over six years ago. They talked for hours while waiting as others began making their way to the airship.

"Wilkins, where have you been all these years?" Finn asked.

"Well, years back when the government *'recruited'* me into service, they began training me as a special operative. There were apparently travelers, foreigners from another world, who were coming to Zanchier. The government wanted people to search for the place that enabled them to come here. After training, we were given a profile on them, and told to find these people."

"Who is we?" Finn asked curiously.

"All of us the government had recruited. There were about a hundred in all."

"Were these strangers dangerous?"

"No, just strangers. All citizens of Zanchier are logged into the databases at birth. Even the poorest of us. These people's bio-scans were not reading. Meaning they weren't from here.

"How many of these strangers were there?"

"About four in total over a period of years, before our S.O. was formed. Sorry, Special Ops," Wilkins clarified.

"They could have been citizens that were just missed," Finn suggested.

"Well, the government didn't think so. They had found and questioned all these people about who they were, where they came from, and how they got here. Anyway, for the first six months they trained us hard, then we were sent out to locate the place that these people said brought them here. From the description of the place that they gave, it was an area in the Xantifal Mountains, high up near the ridge that has storms on a regular basis. These people claimed to have walked out of the storm through a time portal. Well, the government thought that Zanchier was the only place out there. That no other civilizations existed until these people showed up. Time-travel intrigued them, but the uncertainty of it frightened them too, so we were trained by these time-travelers about how to effectively walk through the time portals. When we went into the mountains to find these special storms there were fifty of us on the advanced team that were first to try it. Some of the team members perished or were transported during the Shifts, some of the others were killed by the creatures that live in those mountains, and the remaining twenty-five to thirty of us made it to the ridge. We found the valley where these strangers described as an almost constant barrage of rain and thunderstorms. It was Storm Valley. They said that these storms had brought them here from a place called earth and they were all from different years throughout their planet's timescale."

"You know that this all sounds crazy don't you?"

"Yeah, I thought the same thing too. We all figured them for loons, and the government was spending a ton of Rhedon for nothing. Imagine my surprise when we found that valley and the storms. One of these time-travelers had said that when they exited the portal, there was a Pagorinx in the valley and they chose to go back through the portal to return home instead of facing an extremely large creature. When they turned back, they were spat back out of another portal in the same valley. Only this time the Pagorinx wasn't there."

"Like they were returned to a different time all together but in the same place?"

"Yes, just like that."

"So, these strangers were trapped here?"

"Sort of, yes. Some of the S.O.s tried going through the storms, but they were killed instantly. So, everyone else refused to go. We went back to report our findings, and the government decided to wait a while. Something one of the travelers said was different from the other three. They said they had passed in and out of those same portals several times. The government found that when the seasons change, there is a small window of time where those storms would allow you to leave. When winter was upon us, we could walk through those same storms into other worlds. So, they sent the remainder of the first of the S.O.s back up when winter hit. It was rough going and several more died of exposure to the extreme cold of the Xantifal Mountains. By the time we reached Storm Valley there were only about fifteen of us left. Several walked through and didn't return. So, the rest of us went through the portals into other time periods. Those of us that walked through the same portal on Zanchier came out in the same place, we assume in a different world. We never saw the others again."

"How many were with you?"

"There were eight of us when we started. Some perished in the new worlds we found. Others refused to return to Zanchier. They preferred the strange worlds on the other side. Me, I wanted to come back. I had a family I wanted to return to. But unfortunately, we couldn't find the way back. We tried everything we could. We talked with people of other worlds whose technology mirrored our own here, to see if they could get us home. Most of them wanted to have us institutionalized as loons, but there were very few that we met who knew what we were speaking of. They helped us figure out how to return to our time and place."

"How long were you in these foreign lands, Wilkins?" Finn asked, astonished by his story.

"Almost five years. I found my way home about six months back. I landed in Storm Valley in late fall on the cusp of winter, went in search of my father in Loradin and told him what happened. That's when I found out about Harper and our children. I couldn't go back to the kids without devising a plan first because the government would find me and keep me prisoner until they were done with their questions about where I had been. Then Harper reappeared out of nowhere last week and we've been looking for her ever since."

Finn's mind was blown. The story Wilkins was telling him was a fantastical tale to be certain. Whether or not Finn believed it was going to take some doing on his part. He wasn't one to believe in fairytales, but why would Wilkins lie about all of this? It must be so. One way to find out would be to find some of the other S.O.s and question them. Preferably some that were on the first advanced team. Now that Harper was safe and back home again, his next mission would be exactly that.

"Will," one of the doctors returned and the two of them stood to meet him, "She's waking up. I believe that she will be fine. But no shocks to her system, and she needs plenty of rest. She's been concussed, and we've sealed her wounds to stop the bleeding. But the internal damage will take time."

"Wilkins," Finn said placing a hand on his arm to stop him. "You heard the doctor, no shocks to her system this early in. I know you want to see her, but I suggest that you give her some time."

"You're right. But knowing she's just on the other side of that door is going to be hard."

"Well, when we get back to Loradin, you can focus on getting to know your kids for a while, and I'll focus on getting Harper back in top health. Then when the doctors think she's capable of handling all of this, we'll get you all back together, for good," Finn said with understanding.

Wilkins nodded to Finn as he shook the man's hand. Finn could see his pain at not being able to hold Harper right now. He had been without his wife for six years, and now he had to wait even longer. Wilkins walked away and stood staring out of the windows of the airship. Finn felt for the man. He knew what he was experiencing. Just at that moment, Paisley walked on board the airship, ushering the injured and imprisoned people to a comfortable place.

She looked up to see Finn watching her, a pained look on his face. She straightened and the two of them stood there just looking at each other for a moment before Finn crossed the room, gently sliding his hand around the back of her neck. He planted a kiss on her that made her knees go weak. Once he let go of her, he stood looking into her eyes.

"Goodness, what was that for?" she asked, a slight smile curving the corners of her mouth.

"Life's too short not to. Don't you agree? Sweetheart," he said with a smile.

"Yes. Darling. I heartily agree," she said with a giggle, kissing him back. "I could do this all day, but unfortunately we have a lot of misplaced and injured people to deal with."

"And I need to see about Harper. She's awake but groggy, and surely in pain. I'll see you in a little while," he said, planting another kiss on her forehead.

"I look forward to it," she smiled at him.

Finn grinned to himself while he walked toward the room where Harper was resting. Soon she and Wilkins would be reunited with their children. Not only had Harper almost single-handedly destroyed the Scaithers plans, but she was getting her whole family back. Well almost her whole family. When she found out about her father being the one who betrayed Wilkins and her to the scum of Zanchier, she might just lose it on him. Finn wondered how the gathering of her kids, and possibly her mother as well, had gone. Hopefully, Uncle was able to retrieve them without too much trouble. He supposed they would all soon find out once the airship was loaded, and they all returned to Loradin.

Chapter 16

Reunion

Finn sat patiently by Harper's bed, waiting for his friend to awaken. Her body had ultraviolet light tubes placed upon her injuries to speed the healing process. Her eyelids twitched a tad and he decided to speak to her to see if she would respond.

"Harper?" Finn said in a low soothing voice. Her lids twitched once again, trying to open. He tried again, rubbing her forehead with the thumb of one hand, and her right hand with his other.

Harper's eyes blinked open for a second, as a small smile split the corners of her mouth for a brief second. Finn knew she knew that she was now safe, and that he had found her once again. She reached out and grasped his hand that was covering hers.

Wilkins heart leaped into his throat as he watched the scene through the small window of the door. He was glad that Harper had found someone like Finn who was truly just a friend who cared. He knew the man to be true to his word about their relationship, especially since he had witnessed the display of affection toward Paisley earlier, and her returned affections toward Finn. But watching another man, no matter who it was, console his wife just pained him beyond belief. The government had done so much harm to his little family. Why them, he didn't know. But he would do everything he could to find out when this was all over. At least they would be safe in Loradin for the time being and possibly be able to rebuild their lives.

He turned from the window and went back to find a seat to be alone and just think. His father, Aaric, had communicated to him that they were successful in retrieving the children. Wilkins' parents had both personally gone, both knowing the Fenores. Neitha Brinley had communicated to Gracelynn Fenore about the gravity of the situation.

Gracelynn said she would prepare the children for the move as best she could. The older ones wouldn't be a problem, but Adda might, since she knew no one other than herself and her granddad Derek. Gracelynn decided to send one of their lifetime staff members who all the children were very familiar with along with them to aid the transition for little Adda. She herself turned down the invite for now, stating that her place was with her husband, but that she would be in contact soon. She was given Neitha's personal number for contact should the need arise.

Wilkins decided to take Finn's advice and focus on his children. He would prepare them for their mother's eventual return and regale them with tales of her bravery and strength. By the time Harper *did* return, her children would know her even though they may not remember her.

The airship was finally loaded with their new passengers, the Mods, and Finn's Voyager. Paisley gave orders for lift off, grasping a side handle hanging from the ceiling's edge .

"All right everyone, stay seated until we are airborne and leveled off. We don't want anyone getting off kilter and taking a fall. After the ship has leveled, you're free to move about as you wish. We have some refreshments in the kitchen in the back of the ship to the left, and some bedrolls in storage to lay out in the floor if you wish to rest or sleep. Our flight will be about four hours so make yourselves as comfortable as possible. For those of you with injuries, if the medics haven't already tended to your needs you can see them in the infirmary in the back of the ship on the right."

Finn sat with Harper until he felt the ship level off in the air. She was resting deeply now, so he decided to go see if he could be of any assistance with any of the other rescued prisoners. Vassalage had imprisoned about fifty displaced scientists from all over Zanchier. Two large transports were called in from the airfield to drive those who lived in the outlying areas around Bakrashan and Carpasmere to their homes. The remainder thirty or so extra people were on board the airship. The captain seemed confident that the ship could handle the extra weight, especially since the two transport trucks were no longer on board. The trucks would drive back to Loradin once everyone was seen safely home.

Finn looked around at the people strewn across the floor on bedrolls or wrapped up in large coats and jackets. The rooms were filled with the injured while those who were healthy were in the main area. People slept quietly as the moonlight bathed the dimly lit interior of the airship in a soft glow. Finn noticed Paisley standing by one of the windows. He walked up behind her.

"You all right?" he asked over her shoulder as he stopped beside her.

She looked up at him and half grinned.

"Yes. I was just standing here thinking about that weapon's blast, and the horrible vacuum of circulating storms. I certainly hope that those tornadoes don't leave the area they were in."

"I don't think they will. They sort of looked held there by some force, perhaps created by the void of space which created them in the first place."

"I also wonder if there were any people living in those hills?" she said, looking at Finn with sadness in her eyes.

Finn pulled her into his arms, rubbing her back as she leaned against his chest. "I hope not, Paisley. I really do."

"We'll have to alert all of Zanchier of the dangers of the area. I would say that anything closer than a mile might eventually get sucked into one of the vortexes," she said, leaning back to look up into his face.

"I think one mile is a safe distance, for now. But we'll have to monitor the area closely, indefinitely, just in case anything changes."

Paisley looked into Finn's eyes. "I'm so glad I met you, Finn," she said, leaning her head into his broad chest.

"Me too, sweetheart. Me too."

They stood there for the next ten minutes before breaking up to help tend to those who still needed assistance in some way.

Wilkins stood watch over Harper's door, peeking in through the small window every once in a while just to look at her and make sure she was still sleeping soundly. He didn't know why her father had done what he did to both of them, but that was another thing that he was going to look into. Was Harper's father in league with the Scaither organization, or just a pawn they had used to get what they wanted? Either way, the man had a choice, and he had made the wrong one. Wilkins would never sell-out his family or friends for anything in the world. And since becoming a father himself, he didn't understand how a man could do that to his own child. Especially his only daughter. Wilkins knew that Derek Fenore had never approved of her marrying him, but was that enough to anger him to betray his own family? Wilkins' father was certain, after speaking with Neitha, that Gracelynn knew nothing of the deceit and betrayal by her husband. Wilkins had always liked Gracelynn. His heart hurt for her now that her whole world had been turned upside down once again.

He decided to take a bit and try to find somewhere to lie down for the night. His emotions were raw, he had a headache from all the adrenaline of the night's activities, and his nerves were shot. Wilkins went to the front of the ship, found an unoccupied chair, and tried to sleep. He knew he likely wouldn't but closing his eyes for just a little while might help.

The airship floated easily through the sky, without haste this time, and before they knew it they were back in Loradin, the slightly bumpy landing causing a stirring amongst the lighter sleepers. People began to wake and stretch as they woke others sleeping around them.

Wilkins jumped up from his chair and quickly walked back to Harper's room. She still slept soundly. While he stood there, the medics came to transport her to headquarters medical facilities for further care until they were certain her concussion would not worsen.

"How long will she be in your care?" Wilkins questioned the doctor as he passed.

"We don't really know that yet. As long as she can comprehend what we say and remember people, I'm sure she can be released. Perhaps in a few days."

Wilkins hung his head.

"Will, I know you're anxious, but the shock at seeing you again and her kids, might set her back. It's only a few days longer," the doctor sympathized.

"Yeah doc, only a few days longer huh; we've been apart for six years," Wilkins walked off the ship, jumped into one of the LSS Mods that had been unloaded, and sped off toward his parent's home. Maybe he could at least see his children. Of course, now it was late, and they were probably sleeping, but if they were awake he would sit with them and hold them for as long as they would let him. Then he would pray for Harper's quick recovery so they could return to being a family once more.

Finn watched Wilkins speed away, hoping that he would be all right. Not being able to see Harper was really hard on him. Of course, if Finn were in his shoes, he supposed he would feel the same too. He probably wouldn't have waited and done as he had been told like Wilkins had. He had to hand it to him, he was a stronger man than Finn.

Finn also knew that Harper was going to be very angry when she found out about all of this, but Finn would make sure she understood the sacrifice it had taken for Wilkins to stay away from her.

Finn went in search of Harper, finding the doctors and nurses getting her ready for transport. Finn had never seen Harper look so vulnerable before. She looked tired and weak. He could tell she hurt because of the painful look on her face with each movement of the gurney.

"Hey," Finn said, sticking his head in the room and smiling. "Glad to see you're awake and alert."

"I'm glad *to be* awake and alert. From the way my head feels, I would assume that I've been out of it for a little while?" she said, wincing slightly as they picked her up to carry her out.

"Just the last six hours or so. Although you did wake for a brief moment last night and smile at me."

"Did I? Well, that doesn't sound like me at all. I really did hit my head hard," she teased.

"You are definitely back to your old self as far as your head injury goes," Finn smiled broadly as he slightly chuckled.

"Wait, who are you again?" she looked at him puzzled.

Finn grew serious for a moment and just stared worriedly at Harper.

"Just messing with you, Finn," she smiled.

"That's wrong, Harper," he said, shaking his head at her as they carried her smiling form out the door. "I'll see you in the morning, get some sleep and do what you're told," he yelled after her, her waving hand all he could see of her now.

Finn lowly chuckled, glad she was in good spirits. After the ordeal she had been through she had a right to be angry or feel whatever emotion she wished. Harper's spirit and ability to take whatever life threw at her was what had first drawn him to her.

He helped the others infirmed out to the large transports and aided Paisley and the other agents in the unloading of the airship. A cleanup crew was sent in to deal with the messes while the agents returned home for a well-deserved night's sleep; although, technically, they had done very little. Harper and the other scientists were the true heroes and heroines of this story. The only thing that bothered Finn was the fact that no one had seen Raif Martray. He knew he was there and likely had been the one to fire off that weapon. Where did he get to? Finn would exhaust all the resources he had to find the man who had ruined so many lives. Especially his own.

Wilkins pulled into the driveway of his parents waterfront home on the more unpopulated side of Loradin. He turned the engine off, sat for just a minute, wondering what to say if his children were still awake. He stepped out of the car, took a deep breath, and opened the door to the house. He listened for any activity, not hearing a thing.

"Hello?" Wilkins called out. Still no answer. As he walked through the house, checking rooms as he went, he began to worry that something had happened to them. Paranoia began to take hold as his pace grew until he came to the back-living area that led out into the yard facing the water's edge. There, sitting outside looking up at the stars was his family; his parents and his children. The only one missing was Harper, but hopefully not for long. Wilkins smiled, still a bit frightened at the reaction he might get from them. He stepped through the wall of large, opened doors and out onto the lawn. His mother Neitha saw him coming and stood to welcome him home. The children all watched their newly introduced grandmother. Bain and Seadon vaguely remembered her. She hugged the man who walked out the door. It was a little hard to see who it was, but it didn't take Bain long to recognize his father, beard, and all.

"Dad?" Bain questioned, shocked, slowly standing to look at him to make sure it was him.

"Yeah, Bain. It's me," Wilkins stood there, wanting to scoop them all up but he didn't wish to frighten them.

Bain ran at him and threw his arms around Wilkins as he burst into tears, hugging his father tightly, afraid he might disappear once again. Seadon and Wynne followed Bain's example. Seadon remembered his father as well, and Wynne was happy because she knew he was her father. Tears flowed from every eye there except for little Adda. She sat quietly, hugging Nanny Trea, unsure who all these knew people were.

Wilkins noticed the shy little girl. And after several minutes of hugs, kisses, and tears, he pulled himself away from the other children and went to kneel in front of Adda on the ground. The little girl scooted closer to her nanny, fearful of the man she had never met. Wilkins's heart ached, knowing she had no clue or desire to know who he was.

"Hello, Adda. I know you don't know me, but I would like very much to get to know you. Would that be all right?" He waited patiently on her reply.

Adda looked up at Nanny Trea, a question on her face. Nanny smiled down at her, nodding her head yes to assure the little girl that it would be just fine.

Adda looked back at Wilkins and stood up.

"Hello," she said a bit shyly, then stepped forward and extended her tiny hand for a handshake.

Wilkins eyes filled with tears, as he gently took her hand with his. He wanted to scoop her up and hold her so tightly, but he didn't dare. It was all he could do to keep from bursting into tears. All three of his other children walked up to him and Adda and knelt down beside them, wrapping their arms around their sister and father, reassuring Adda that this was daddy, and he was okay to love. So, Adda reached out and wrapped her arms around Wilkins' neck. They stayed outside well into the early morning hours, catching up with all that Wilkins had missed over the years as his children excitedly talked about their lives. Bain sat to his right, with Seadon sitting at his feet. His beautiful Wynne curled up next to his left and his little Adda, wrapped up in a blanket, securely curled up in his arms. The only thing that could make it more perfect was having Harper right beside him.

Soon Wilkins, he thought. *Soon.*

Chapter 17

Another Reunion

Harper lay in the medic wing at the LSS headquarters looking out at the harbor far off in the distance. She really didn't know who these people were, how Finn was involved, or where she was except for the small amount of information the doctors and nurses gave her.

The doctor said he didn't want to overload her brain at the moment and that she just needed to rest and relax until she felt much better. Then everything would be explained.

At least she had a room with a very nice view. She laid there watching ships come in and out of the harbor, going through some sort of checkpoint. She knew she was in Loradin, but how that was possible was a shock. The Loradin government was very choosy about who came in. Finn must really have some major contacts.

Someone knocked, and the door to her room opened. She turned her head to see who it might be. Finn walked in smiling at her.

"Looks like you're feeling quite well?"

"I am. I just wish I could get out of here. I mean, the view is nice, and all the relaxation has been great, but I'm crazy bored."

"You've been in here for a little over thirty-six hours," Finn said with raised eyebrows.

"It feels like a week," she stated, pushing herself into an upright position, grimacing slightly.

"It might just end up taking that long, so quit your bellyaching and accept the terms," he said, grinning as he sat on the bed's edge. Just as he sat down there was another knock at the door. They both looked as Kamsten Whitsler came in.

"Kamsten?" Harper smiled as the woman came over and hugged her neck. "What are you doing here?"

"It's Finn's fault. No wait, I take that back. Actually, it's your fault," she grinned. "The powers that be over here in Loradin were so impressed with my skills at altering people's appearances, aka, you, that they begged me to come work for them. By the way, we need to change you back, and soon."

"Why?" Harper asked puzzled, "what if I like my new looks?" she teased.

"You might like them, but your kids might want to see their mother, not a stranger looking back at them," Kamsten stated without thinking.

"What?" Harper sat upright in bed, ignoring the pain the sudden movement caused, glancing back and forth between the two of them.

Finn looked at Kamsten with a reprimanding stare.

"Oops, sorry. I thought someone already told you," she said. "I'm just gonna' go now. Harper, I'll see you a bit later." Kamsten ducked her head and quickly left the room before Finn gave her a boot in the rear.

"Finn, what is she talking about?" Harper asked wide-eyed.

"Harper, calm down. We weren't supposed to say anything until the doctor thought you could handle the excitement. Your concussion is pretty bad you know."

Harper's eyes filled with tears, "Finn, are my kids here?"

"Not in the building, no. But they are in Loradin. I don't think their grandparents told them about you yet."

"My parents are here too?" she asked confused.

"Not exactly. Okay. Before we get into all this I want you to sit back, relax and listen to what I am going to tell you as calmly as you can. All right?" Finn said sternly. "The doctor is probably going to rip me for this."

Harper shook her head yes, and leaned back against the pillows, trying to relax.

"Now, are you ready?" Finn asked, watching her. "If I see you getting too excited I'm going to stop."

"Okay," Harper said as she breathed deeply.

"When you were taken again, the LSS, which stands for Loradin Secret Society, —the people who take care of the bad guys without the world knowing about it— found out who you were. They then recruited me and Kamsten to work for them. The person who heads up this special group is known as Uncle and happens to be your father-in-law."

Finn noticed Harper's eyes grow wide. "You okay? Should I keep going? You aren't getting dizzy or feeling overloaded or anything are you?"

"No. Please continue," Harper clipped out.

"Well, they found where you were being held and put together a group of people to rescue you and the others being held at Vassalage. Your father-in-law figured that your children might be in danger if we succeeded, so he and your mother-in-law contacted your mother and made arrangements to collect the children and bring them back here where they could be protected by the Loradian government. Your in-laws have been wanting to see you but were unsure if you could handle it yet." Finn stopped and waited for Harper to process everything he had told her so far, choosing not to mention Wilkins just yet. They knew the children might slip and say something about him, so they were going to let them all see her at the same time. Finn might try and give her a hint just before, so it isn't a complete overload, but not until the day it was to happen.

"So, I get to have my children back?" She teared up and her voice began to crack.

"Yes, and you're all to live here in Loradin with Aaric and Neitha until you choose to get your own place. You will all be safe here and can live normal lives."

"Oh Finn," Harper said, placing her hands over her nose and mouth as tears streamed down her cheeks. "Thank you, for everything you have ever done for me, thank you."

"You are very welcome, Harper. I wouldn't have had it any other way," he said, reaching out and taking her hand in his.

Another knock on the door and in walked the doctor. He took one look at the teary-eyed Harper, then looked at Finn with a stern questioning face.

"Kamsten let slip about the *children* and I had to fill in the rest," Finn said, emphasizing '*children*' when he spoke, hoping the doctor caught the lack of reference concerning Wilkins.

"All right then." He turned his attention to Harper. "How are you feeling this morning, Harper. Any dizziness, headaches, nausea, can you remember everything about your life, family, friends?" he questioned as he shined a light into her eyes, checked her wounds and did some other regular tests.

"I feel fine doctor. I have none of those symptoms, but I haven't been able to stand up yet. The only pain I feel is a little soreness or pulling where the shrapnel hit me. And yes, I remember everything about my life, no matter how unfortunate some of it was."

The doctor finished his exam, stood, and looked between the both of them.

"I'm going to release you from the medic facility, but" he emphasized when he saw the excitement on Harper's face. "I expect you to take it very easy and you cannot stay alone for at least a week, just to make sure you have no other concussion symptoms. Is that understood?" he asked, looking back and forth between the both of them.

"I'll make sure she obeys every rule, Doc. I promise," Finn stated, staring Harper down.

"So do I. As long as I can get out of here and see my children?" Harper pleaded.

"I really wish you'd give it another day or two," the doctor said. "With your internal injuries, I'm afraid the excitement of the reunion might open up a wound."

Harper began shaking her head wildly in protest as the doctor spoke. Finn held up his hand to Harper, looking at her to calm her down. She knew Finn understood and would take her side in the matter, so she did just that. She calmed down and just listened.

"Doc, I will not make her wait any longer than I have to. I will talk with the children first and explain that their mother needs to be handled with the utmost care, and that they will have to be easy and gentle with her," Finn said firmly.

"Fine, do as you see fit. But, if you have any problems, come right back here. Understand?" he stated.

"Yes!" Harper answered excitedly.

"I'll have the nurse come take the needles out. After that, you're free to go."

Harper looked at Finn; excitement making her nerves a jumbled mess.

"Harper stay right in that bed until that nurse comes. And don't leave this room until I get back. I'm just going out in the hall to make a com-call and I'll be back as soon as I can. Stay right here, you understand?" he threatened her with a look.

"Yes, Finn. I promise. Right here till you get back," she said honestly, so happy and anxious she could hardly bear it.

Harper looked up and clasped her hands together as she had often seen Finn do. "Finn says that you're real. If you are, thank you for bringing me back to my children. And if you can, please bring Wilkins back to us too."

The nurse came in soon after with an armload of clothing for Harper. She unhooked her from the machines and helped her get herself dressed. Harper stood at the window looking out over the city below. Impressed with the beauty of it all and glad to be able to call it home.

Finn walked the corridor outside Harper's room as he spoke with Wilkins.

"The doctor let her go, and I will bring her home using one of the Mods. I haven't told her about you yet. I figured that could be a surprise for her, so let me bring her in and sit her down before you all reveal yourselves. And make sure the children know that they need to be very gentle with her."

"Finn," Wilkins voice almost broke over the com-call, "thank you, for everything."

"You and Harper sure are an appreciative sort," Finn joked, "Be there in a couple of hours or so. We need to see Kamsten first to change her appearance back so the kids will know her."

Wilkins clicked the call closed and stood there in joyful shock unable to move. Tears of joy ran down his cheeks as he sunk to the floor.

Bain walked in and saw him and concern washed over him.

"Dad? Are you all right?" he asked, kneeling down beside him.

Wilkins gathered his composure and hugged his wonderful son.

"I'm great son. Your mother will be on her way here in a few hours," he told him as he stood. Bain grinned as Wilkins hugged him.

"Let's go tell your brother and sisters, but there are some rules to obey. I'll explain once everyone is seated in the living room."

"All right, Harper. Are you ready?" Finn asked as he held the medic room door open.

"I've been ready for this for years," she grinned nervously.

Finn wheeled her and the wheelchair the doctor insisted she use down to Kamsten's laboratory.

"We need to fix you back to your old self first," Finn clarified.

"Right, I forgot about that," Harper stated.

"Harper," Kamsten smiled at her, "are you ready for your transformation back to the real you?"

"Yes, whatever I need to do to see my children quicker," she said, getting aggravated that it was taking so long.

"I think this would be best. Especially where Adda is concerned," Finn clarified.

Harper sighed. Finn always knew best and thought of the bigger picture.

"You're right, Finn. I'm just anxious."

"I know, and as soon as Kam's done, we'll go straight there."

Kamsten dyed Harper's hair back to its original red, bio-scanned her skin to the pale, slightly freckled flesh tone she was born with, and pigmented her eyes to her original green.

After an hour in Kamsten's laboratory, Harper looked in the mirror, recognizing herself, but missing the person she had seen staring back at her for the last three years.

"Are you ready, Harper?" Finn asked, jarring her from her study of the person in the mirror.

"Yes, very much so," she said. "But I'm walking to the Module," she insisted.

Finn grinned at her resolve and pushed the wheelchair aside.

He led her to the Mod parking garage where he had a Module ready and waiting. He helped her slide into the seat and then took up the wheel and steered them to the Brinley's home.

Everyone was there waiting on her, including Wilkins' parents and Nanny Trea. These last two groups would hold off until Wilkins and the children got to be reunited with Harper.

Twenty minutes after leaving the LSS medical facility they pulled into the Brinley driveway. Harper breathed deeply and exhaled. Finn looked at her, grabbed her hand and gave it a squeeze.

"It'll be okay Harper. The children have already been briefed about your condition. We'll take everything as slowly as you like."

"I'm okay, Finn. It's all just a bit surreal. I've been planning this day for so long and now it's here." Harper opened the door and climbed out, not waiting on Finn. He had to hurry and run to the other side afraid she might take off running.

They approached the door and knocked. Neitha and Aaric answered the door together, welcoming Harper with open arms.

"Harper, come in dear," Neitha instructed. Finn and Aaric followed behind as Neitha led her to the living room and sat her on the couch. She and Aaric disappeared and soon returned with the children. Bain was in front and ran to her when he saw her, careful to hug her gently. Seadon followed behind, with Wynne holding hands with Adda, to introduce the little girl to their mother. Harper's emotions got the better of her as she cried and laughed at the same time as her children gently sat beside her, hugging her, and crying too. Little Adda stood in front of her mother, placed her hands on either side of her face and looked at Harper.

"Mama?" Adda asked with a grin.

Harper smiled and cried all at once as she reached out and hugged her tightly. She looked at Neitha with questioning eyes.

"We've been showing them old photographs of you that we had here; even where you were pregnant with her," Neitha explained.

Finn had been right. Changing her appearance back had been the right move. She sat holding her children and crying for about five minutes, before looking up at the others gathered in the room. Her eyes stopped on Wilkins and her breath caught in her throat.

"Wilkins," she barely squeaked out as the children moved aside and she stood, weeping so hard that her entire body shook with each sob and step that she took. She limped across the room as he hurriedly walked toward her. She threw her arms around his neck as he wrapped his around her, trying not to squeeze too tightly, cradling her head in one of his hands. They stood sobbing as they held onto each other. Wilkins motioned to the kids to join them as all six of them wrapped up in an embrace that was long overdue. The rest of the onlookers walked out of the room to give them all a little privacy and went outside to wait for them to make their way to join them. If they didn't choose to do so, then they would all rejoice together in the morning.

Chapter 18

Betrayed

Harper woke, her body sore from the injuries. She remembered last night and looked around, smiling at the bodies of her children strewn all around her. She felt the steady breathing of someone else. She turned her head to look up into the face of Wilkins, sleeping soundly beside her, his arms locked around her protectively as her head rested on his chest. Tears stung her eyes once again as the joy that she felt, and the release of all the pent-up anxiety from the years that her little family suffered broken, separated, and lonely, flowed out of her.

Wilkins stirred awake, feeling someone watching him. He opened his eyes to the face of his beautiful wife. Tears escaped her eyes and rolled down her cheeks. He stroked them away with his thumb as they lay there on the floor wrapped in each-other's arms, looking at one another.

Adda began to stir and woke, looking around the room. She sat up, crawled over to them, and lay down between them snuggling as close to them both as she could. Harper and Wilkins both smiled ear to ear as they each stroked their baby's hair. Tears of joy fell down both of their cheeks as they lay there holding each other and Adda. The rest of the kids woke, looked at their parents, and did the same, all piling up around them tightly. Harper and Wilkins kissed each other, smiled at the pile all around them, legs and arms thrown over their own, and happily went back to sleep.

Aaric, Neitha, and Trea stood watching the quiet interaction, all wiping away silent tears. Trea turned to go and cook breakfast, Neitha agreeing to meet her in a moment. They would make a breakfast feast fit for a king. Neitha grabbed several blankets, covered the sleeping miracles as best she could, and left the room.

Several hours later the first of the stragglers entered the kitchen. Bain, soon followed by Seadon, and Wynne, approached the island and sat down.

"Trea, we're starving. I think we missed dinner last night," Bain stated.

"I believe you did. With all the excitement last night, no one wanted to eat," Trea answered. "Just have a seat. We made a whole mess of things for breakfast this morning. What do you all want? You just tell Nanny Trea, and I'll tend to it."

The three kids all looked at each other with confused expressions. Trea had always been sternly friendly, but today she was downright cheerful. Seadon asked what they were all thinking.

"Nanny Trea, are you feeling all right?"

"Well of course I am! Why do you ask such a question?" she replied, curiously.

"Well," Wynne began, always having a way with words, "You're, umm, happier than usual. You've always been kind," she rushed to say. "But today you're very… happy," the young girl replied carefully.

"Well, I'm just happy for you children is all. You all have your mother and father back. It's a happy day indeed," she said crying again.

Little Adda stood in the doorway of the kitchen, "Nan Trea, why are you sad?"

"Oh for goodness sakes!" Trea said, wiping the tears from her eyes and smiling. "Come here child. There's no sadness in Nan Trea. These are happy tears."

"You mean like mother's and father's happy tears last night and this morning?" she asked, rubbing the sleep from her eyes.

"Yes, exactly like that," Trea said, tickling the girl under her chin. "Now, what will you have for breakfast, little one?"

"Pancakes!" she squealed.

When Harper and Wilkins woke again, all the children were gone. They could hear them in the kitchen, laughing with each other and Nan Trea.

Harper and Wilkins lay on the floor on their sides, facing each other. Their noses were almost touching as they studied each other's faces. Another giggle erupted from the kitchen and they both smiled.

"That's a beautiful sound," Wilkins said, lazily grinning.

Harper giggled at the look of joy on his face. "I love you Wilkins. So much," she said, one lone joyful tear streaking down her cheek and hitting the carpet beneath.

"Now *that's* even more beautiful," he said, pulling her closer to him and holding her tightly as they kissed; both afraid they might wake, and it would all have been a dream. They simply laid there in each other's arms, relishing the feeling of one another, and the sounds emanating from the kitchen.

"Where have you been all this time, Will?" Harper asked, unaccusingly.

"It's a very long and strange tale, Harper. One that we don't have time to discuss this morning. I'll just say that I was somewhere that I couldn't get back to you. I finally made it back six months ago and found out about you and the kids. I've been searching for you ever since."

"Why do you think this happened to us Will?"

"I have several theories, but nothing definitive."

"Well, we can think about all that later. Right now, what do you say about going and having breakfast with our children?"

"That sounds like an amazing idea. I'm starving actually," Wilkins said, standing and gently pulling her to her feet.

She grimaced slightly. Wilkins looked at her and asked, "Harper, are you all right?"

"Yeah, just a bit sore from sleeping on the floor all night, but I wouldn't have had it any other way," she smiled.

"Well, tonight we sleep in a bed. Mom has all the rooms made up and taken care of."

"As much as I wish to be alone with you, if all of our children come climb in bed with us, I won't kick them out," she stated, a pleading look in her eyes.

"Don't worry. Neither could I," he said. They both grinned, walking into the kitchen with arms wrapped around each other's waist.

They sat next to one another at the kitchen island where their children were setting having their breakfast, joining in with the camaraderie, still unable to let go of one another.

Aaric and Neitha stood at the top of the staircase arm in arm, looking down over the scene below them. Their home was complete once again. Not only had they gotten their son back, but their daughter-in-law and all their grandchildren as well.

Neitha sighed, "I hope this lasts forever, Aaric,"

"As do I, dear. But I'm afraid we might still have some rough patches to deal with," Aaric sighed. "We still have to tell Harper about her father's involvement in all of this."

"Do we really need to tell her, Aaric?" Neitha asked, worried about how it might affect her.

"I'm afraid so, Neitha. She deserves to know the truth. She's been through hell and back over the last six years. They all have." Aaric kissed his wife's cheek, "How about we worry about all of this later and go join our family for breakfast."

She smiled at her husband, and the two of them walked downstairs to join in the merriment of the moment.

After breakfast was over, Wilkins and Harper took the children outside along the water's edge to walk the small rocky shoreline made by the Loradian government. Nan Trea packed them a picnic lunch to take with them so they wouldn't have to rush back home. The late winter days were beginning to warm as spring was just around the corner, so they shouldn't get too cold if they spent the day outdoors.

Aaric left to go to the office, while Neitha retreated to her room to take a com-call from Gracelynn Fenore.

"Hello Gracelynn," Neitha said.

"Neitha, how is Harper and Wilkins, and the children?"

"They're just fine, Gracelynn. A happy reunion all around."

"Are they all well? Health wise I mean. I've heard about some of those government forced prisons and how they treat those being held there."

"Other than Harper's injuries, I'd say she is doing very well."

"Injuries? What Injuries? Neitha, please tell me what's been happening. Derek won't tell me a thing. He says he doesn't know, but I'm sure he's hiding something from me. I haven't had the benefit of asking my daughter because as soon as she resurfaced she disappeared again."

"Are you certain you want to know, Gracelynn? It isn't a pretty story."

"No matter what the story is, Neitha, I have a right to know. She's my daughter and Wilkins is my son-in-law. I've raised those children for the last five years as my own and now I'm left with absolutely nothing. Please, Neitha, tell me what's happened, and why, if you know."

Neitha Brinley sighed heavily, "All right, Gracelynn, but don't say I didn't warn you." The two women sat and talked for the next hour as Neitha informed her of all she knew, including Derek's expected involvement in the disappearance of both Wilkins and Harper, his shady dealings with the likes of Commander Raif Martray, and Vonder Mortruff, and his involvement with Harper's disappearance again at the Winterfest.

As the children played along the shoreline, Harper and Wilkins talked about his experience with the S.O. team and the places he discovered on the other side of the portal.

Harper related all that had happened to her over the years since he disappeared from their lives. The places she lived, including how they must have just missed each other at the ridge line of the Xantifal Mountains.

"Harper, I was at Vassalage when we found you. Finn and I found you lying outside after the weapon caught fire and exploded, injuring you. The doctor's wouldn't let me see you until he thought you could handle the stress of seeing me. Everyone thought I would be too big of a shock for you, so I did as I was told. That was the hardest thing I've ever had to do, watching you lie there in that room, just a few feet away, unable to touch you or hold you. I thought I was going to go crazy. So, I came here, met the kids for the first time and made sure they knew their mother was one brave, tough woman. You do know you basically single-handedly wiped out the Scaither's plans to destroy Zanchier and its people?"

Harper looked at Wilkins, understanding having to be so close but not being able to interact. Just like she did with their children at Winterfest. She touched his cheek and leaned her forehead against his. Then she thought about what he said about her being a heroin.

"Wilkins, I was the one who finished that weapon for them in the first place. I just wanted my life to get back to normal. We all stalled as long as we could but Martray was growing wise to us. When I saw what that weapon did to the landscape it frightened me so much that I couldn't let it happen again. Wilkins, what if there were people who lived there? Other families like ours who are gone now?" Harper shuddered at the thought.

"You can't do that to yourself, Harper. You were doing the best that you could. And you stopped it from happening again. None of this is your fault. This is the fault of the men behind the corruption of the government. Men like Raif Martray, Vonder Mortruff, and others."

"Others being my father?" Harper asked, looking out over the water and her children playing at the edge.

"I'm sorry, Harper, but yes. The LSS has been watching all of them for the last year or so. When you appeared at the party, Dad was shocked. Then Paisley informed him that your father was the one who turned you over to Martray. He was involved with both of our disappearances years ago."

Harper's head snapped around to look at Wilkins. "My father did this to us?" she asked, astonished. "Why?" came the anguished cry. Harper's eyes filled with tears again. "Did my mother know too?"

"No. I'm certain that Gracelynn was innocent and unaware of everything that your father was involved with. She didn't know about any of it. I can't imagine what would cause a man to do what he did. Maybe they threatened him, or Gracelynn, or our kids unless he cooperated with whatever they wanted from him?"

"That's no excuse, Will. I can't believe he did all of that or helped with it. I have been put through living hell over the last six years and my own father was part of it."

Wilkins held Harper while she cried once more over the shock of being so betrayed by the one man who should have always protected and taken care of her.

"Will, I'm so tired. Tired of living like this. I'm ready for a quiet, normal life where we raise our kids as normal citizens of Zanchier."

"We *were* normal citizens of Zanchier.. Other than your brilliant mind and my ownership of a rich mineral deposit, we were normal. We never know what can happen, as you well know. We just have to hang on and pray we make it through. We've won the last battle, and no matter what, I will find my way to you again, no matter where either of us end up. If we hide away with our kids, what kind of life would that be for them?"

"I know, Wilkins, I understand what you're saying. But a few years in a hideaway would be really nice," she said smiling, knowing full well it would never happen.

"I agree, but it isn't possible. Bain is nearly old enough to join the work force. Seadon wants to go to the Airship Academy in Praxtingen. That's a boarding academy. Even though he now wants to wait a little longer since we've all been reunited. Wynne isn't sure what she's good at. Seclusion would be awful for her."

"How do you already know so much about them?"

"I had a full day and a half with them before you came home. Kids can talk. A lot!" he chuckled as Harper laughed along with him.

"Will, I need to confront my father. He has to know that I know what he did to us."

"If you're sure that's what you want, then we can leave as soon as you want."

"It is. I want to get it over with. Can we go tomorrow?"

"I'll ask dad about using the airship. We can make it a family event. The kids can see their friends, supervised of course, and we can deal with your father."

Wilkins com-called his father with the request and received a yes. Twenty agents would accompany them. Three agents per family member, give or take. Finn and Paisley insisted on going along as two of them.

The next day, the airship was boarded, and the trip to Everly-Sound began. Seadon was invited inside the control room with the captain and mates. He was even allowed to momentarily steer the airship, and the captain was truly impressed at his knowledge of flight already. He assured him of an apprenticeship under his own tutelage once he finished the academy. Bain was interested in joining the LSS after he discovered what it was they did. And since his grandfather ran it, he was a shoe-in. They enjoyed their first family trip together since their separation; floating high above Zanchier. They would reach Everly-Sound in a little under two and a half hours, and Harper would confront her father and that would be the last time she would ever see him again. After that, she and her family would move on to better days and try to forget the horrors of the past.

Chapter 19

The Confrontation

Gracelynn Fenore sat in the garden outside her home in Everly-Sound while Derek was away at work. She was overwhelmed by all she had learned from Neitha Brinley on the phone this morning and had spent the last several hours crying so much it made her sick. She had no idea that Derek was involved in so much. Her own husband had hurt their own family more than any one man ever should. Did she ever really know him? She felt as though the man Neitha described, and the man she had spent the last thirty-seven years married to, were two completely different people. She never would have seen any of what Neitha told her. She had trusted him. How could he have done what he did to Harper, or to her?

Gracelynn knew Harper was coming tomorrow to confront her father. Neitha had been good enough to give her a heads up about the impromptu visit, after which Gracelynn would be packed and ready to leave with them back to Loradin. She would never be able to trust Derek again, and frankly she could barely stand to look at the man. Her whole life had been one big lie and she had been the last to know about it.

She had only herself to blame for her ignorance. In the past when she had questioned Derek about his business dealings he would simply kiss her on the forehead and tell her not to worry herself with the business. He would handle everything so she and Harper wouldn't have to. She thought he was being a good husband in this way, but he was hiding his crooked dealings from her. She should have insisted on knowing what he was involved with. Now, it was too late.

Gracelynn took the rest of the day to get her personal affairs in order. She went to the bank and cashed out her accounts, putting the rhedon aside in a travel bag. She would not be destitute after thirty-seven years of trusting her husband to take care of her and their child. Derek owed her much more than she took. She didn't even take what she should have, but she would be comfortable for the remainder of her life as a single woman. She didn't want to start over at fifty-five, but she refused to live in misery forever.

Derek Fenore, was sweating bullets this morning, knowing that Raif Martray and Vonder Mortruff would be stopping by his home office some time that evening. He wasn't sure what they were upset about, but he knew it was major. He had never met with Martray before, only Mortruff. He didn't know what else they expected from him. He had lied to everyone he knew, sacrificed his daughter and her husband to the cause, fearful that they would come after the rest of the family. Now, it appeared that it had all been in vain. He was certain that things had gone badly, and they were coming after him for whatever reasons. Derek would leave his city office early today, swing by the bank, and start to get things ready for him and Gracelynn to disappear before Martray and Mortruff could show up. The grandchildren were already moved to a safe place, meaning someone knew something major was about to happen. He didn't know what, but he wouldn't wait around to find out. As he threw some important papers in his satchel there was a knock at his office door. He nervously looked up to see whom he assumed to be Raif Martray, Vonder Mortruff and several other men not waiting for an invite, enter his office. Derek went white as a sheet as fear and realization overtook him.

Harper and Wilkins, nervously and through great assurance that they would be safe, gave the children two hours to visit with friends and then meet back at the airship by noon. They were given explicit instructions to stay close to their LSS agents. They were, under no circumstances, to be out of their line of vision for any reason whatsoever. Neitha and Nan Trea would stay on board with Adda, while the others visited friends. Wynne chose to stay on board as well, not really having any close friends to visit with anyway. The only person she wanted to see was Grandmother Gracelynn, and Neitha had informed her that she was coming to stay with them for a while. Harper had overheard this conversation and put two and two together to figure out what it meant. Her mother was leaving her father. Surely due to his horrid betrayal and the years of lies and deceit.

Harper, Wilkins, Aaric, Finn, Paisley, and four other agents all headed out to Everly-Sound to retrieve her mother and confront her father.

As they drove to the island, Harper went over and over in her head what she would say to him.

When they arrived, the house seemed empty. Her mother's driver was not there. One of the Fenore's long time maids answered the door.

"Miss Harper! Mr. Wilkins! My goodness, it's so good to see you both!"

"Hello Francine. Is Mother or Father home?"

"Mrs. Gracelynn left for town this morning. She did say she would be back by 11 a.m. for certain and to tell Mr. Fenore that she wanted to speak to him immediately and not to leave."

"So is Mr. Fenore here?"

"Yes ma'am. Mr. Fenore is in his office. He has been home for several hours and hasn't come out of his office since arriving."

"Is something wrong?"

"I'm not certain ma'am. We haven't checked on Mr. Fenore because he always rings when he needs something. We aren't allowed in his study without his permission under any circumstances."

"Yes, I remember all too well that rule. Thank you, Francine."

Harper and the others walked the long, wide, tall hallway toward Derek's office. Harper was just about to knock on the door when Gracelynn walked through the front door.

"Harper?" Gracelynn yelled, running to meet her daughter. She grabbed Harper in a fierce hug and cried.

Harper cried right along with her mother. They stood there for a minute happy in their reunion. Harper finally pulled away to compose herself.

"Mom, as much as I love this, we have important business to tend to."

"I know, sweetheart. I just, I've just missed you. Oh, and Wilkins." Gracelynn let go of Harper to hug her long-lost son-in-law.

Harper turned to Aaric and the others. "I would like to speak to my father alone first. Mother and I, that is. We both have a lot to say to Father."

Aaric said, "Fine Harper. We'll be right here if you need us."

Wilkins asked, "Are you sure you don't want me to come in with you?"

"I'm sure, Will. This is something we need to do ourselves."

Harper and Gracelynn turned toward the large oak doors, and without knocking, walked into her father's office, and shut the doors behind them.

Derek Fenore sat at his desk, his head in his hands. He was so lost in thought that he hadn't heard his office doors open. When he heard the click of the doors closing, he looked up to see who would have the nerve to enter his office unannounced? His face fell in shock and his heart stopped beating for a second.

"Harper?" His words were little more than a whisper. Derek scrambled to get up, his body ached, and one eye was swollen shut. He limped around his desk, holding his large stomach with his left hand. "My goodness, girl, where have you been…"

Harper held up her hand to stop him. "Don't father. I know what you did to me and Wilkins. Don't pretend."

"I…I…don't know what you're talking about," Derek stuttered.

Gracelynn stepped forward at that, fuming mad. "How dare you, Derek! How could you? How could you *sell* your own family, you're only daughter, her husband, you're grandchildren, to those evil men?"

"Now Gracelyn, you don't know what you're talking about…"

"Oh, I know exactly what you did. And everything you're involved in. I see that it is starting to catch up to you," Gracelynn said, looking over the beaten and battered appearance of her husband.

Harper stepped up. "Why father? Was my marrying Wilkins so bad? Did you feel so betrayed that you would allow my family to be ripped apart. In that prison, they beat me so severely sometimes that I had to spend days recovering."

"Now, Harper, they had explicit instructions to not lay a hand on you."

"Really? So, you allowed my kidnapping, as long as they didn't beat me?" Harper asked in astonishment. Derek began backing away toward his desk as Harper moved forward, her anger evident.

"It wasn't like that…"

"What was it like, father? You allowed them to take my husband…"

"That, I had nothing to do with."

"But you knew who was responsible and allowed it to happen," Harper said, astonishment and pain evident in her voice and expression.

"Well, yes, sort of. You're twisting the whole situation. You have no idea what I have to deal with in my position in the government."

Gracelynn became very angry at his statement. "How dare you!"

Harper and Derek turned to look at her at her exclamation. Gracelynn walked up to Derek, nearly nose to nose with him. "How dare you use your business dealings and problems as an excuse to do what you've done to our family! It's outrageous, Derek. I thought I knew you. I trusted you. I loved you."

Derek's face fell at her words. She loved him, she said. Past tense. He had lost Gracelynn.

"Gracey..." he began to beg.

"Don't call me that! You can never use that name for me again. As a matter of fact, once I walk out those doors, I never want to see, or speak to you again."

Derek fell back into his chair at his desk at her words. He never thought that she would turn on him. "But... you're my wife."

"I *was* you're wife, Derek. A wife that trusted you. I would have done nearly anything for you. You lied to me our entire marriage. You *took* my only child from me, Derek. I'll never forgive you for what you've done to us."

Harper waited until her mother was finished before she began again.

"I don't know why you did what you did, father. But just know, Wilkins and I are together again. And, we have our children back. You took *six years* of my life father. My baby doesn't even know who I am. They told me she had died. I had no idea she was alive. I mourned her loss, and the loss of my husband and other three children for years! I just want to know why?"

Derek looked at the pain on his daughters face. The bruises, the cuts, and scrapes on her body. He thought about what Vonder and Raif said to him as their lackeys beat him that very morning. Blaming him for what Harper had done to ruin their plans. Threatening Gracelynn's life and promising to return later and finish him off if he didn't get his house in order and control his daughter.

"They threatened us, Harper. They're going to kill your mother and me, and likely the children as well."

"That's a coward's excuse father. If you had never gotten mixed up with them in the first place you wouldn't have had to deal with this now. I just want to let you know that after today, I'll not dwell on you again. Think of you, yes. You are my father. But you hurt me beyond belief, and I'll put your memory behind me. And you don't have to worry about Mother or the children. We will all be somewhere we can't be touched."

Derek looked pleadingly at Gracelynn. "Gracelynn… come with me. I'm ready to leave. I was packing for you and me to disappear. I was just waiting for you to get home. We can go somewhere and start over."

"Oh, *I'm* going somewhere to start over, Derek. It just isn't with you. I'm going with our daughter, son-in-law, and our grandchildren. Goodbye, Derek."

As Gracelynn and Harper left Derek's office, he sat behind his desk, stunned that his life could change so drastically all in one day. He watched his wife and daughter walk out the door as Aaric Brinley appeared in the doorway, followed by some other people with weapons.

One of the men approached him and said, "Derek Fenore, you're under arrest for crimes against the people of Zanchier, kidnapping, and an accomplice to murder."

"Murder? Now hold on, I never murdered anyone!"

Aaric stepped up. "You may not have committed the crime yourself, Derek. But you supported those that did. You had a hand in so much. You're lucky I don't kill you myself for what you did to my son and his family."

"Aaric, you have to understand. You don't know what these men are capable of!" Derek pleaded and yelled as they walked him out of the house and the front door. They loaded him into the Mod and drove him to the airship and put him into lock-up.

Wynne and Adda watched their grandfather being walked through the ship in handcuffs. He looked at them with regret as tears of shame began to streak his cheeks.

"Grandfather?" Adda called shyly, as Nan Trea scooped her into her arms, trying to divert her attention to the scenery outside. Wynne sat with Neitha and cried as her grandmother wrapped her arms comfortingly around

Wynne's shoulders. Wynne knew then that her grand- father had done something terribly wrong.

Harper, Wilkins, and the others returned shortly after, boarding the airship. When Adda saw Gracelynn appear on the airship, she yelled her name and wiggled her way out of Nan Trea's arms, running to her grandmother. Gracelynn scooped the little girl up.

"Oh, my little Adda. How I've missed you." Wynne ran over to Gracelynn too, throwing her arms around the woman's waist.

Adda asked her, "Why did those men have grandfather in handcuffs?"

"Well, my sweet. Your grandfather did some very bad things and he must go away for a while to make amends for the horrible things he did."

"Why did he do horrible things?"

"Oh, Adda, if I only knew the answer to that." She kissed the little girl and squeezed Wynne at her side. Harper and Wilkins walked over to the trio and threw their arms around them. They all stood there for a few minutes together, just loving on each other.

The boys soon returned, both happy to see their grandmother Gracelynn. They asked where their grand-father was, so Harper and Wilkins took them aside to explain what had happened. Bain knew what Derek had done already, but Seadon was a bit upset by the news.

The airship was soon airborne and headed back to Loradin, and to the safety and new beginning of their new lives.

Raif Martray and Vonder Mortruff sat and watched the scene before them from a safe, undetectable distance. They watched the LSS agents take Derek Fenore on board the airship in handcuffs. Raif noticed his old friend Finn Mobley, wondering if he knew yet that he had been the one to order his family killed. If Raif knew Aaric Brinley, he was certain Finn had been briefed on all the news by now. His attention turned to Harper, Wilkins, and Gracelynn, as they walked on board as well. He fumed angrily, his face contorting in hatred as he watched Harper walk up the steps, arm in arm with Wilkins.

She had destroyed his plans, and now he would have to think of another way to accomplish the takeover of all of Zanchier. He only wished that he and Vonder had Derek Fenore killed instead of beaten. The man would talk and tell the LSS everything. No matter, Raif was above all of them. They couldn't get close enough to him to catch him. He was too well protected by those in power that he held in his grasp. His plans were too far gone for it to be undone now. Too many things had transpired, and he would soon control all the Zanchieths of Bakrashan and Carpasmere. The only place he hadn't been able to corrupt yet was Loradin. He had all the resources of all the other cities at his fingertips, and he would use them to destroy Loradin. He would figure out a way to breach that city if it were the last thing he did.

Vonder would make sure Riglan was trained and ready to take over his vast empire one day. He was a fairly smart boy after-all and took after Vonder in every aspect of the word. Vonder always talked about how proud he was of his only son, and how Riglan would soon be ready to graduate academy and be given responsibilities within the Mortruff organization. Raif hoped the boy was ready and willing to do what was necessary, because this little hiccup with Harper and the weapon was merely a temporary setback. Raif grinned menacingly at Vonder as he started his Mod and they drove away.

Chapter 20

Finding Home

Aaric and Neitha's large home was packed and noisy, and they couldn't be happier about it.

Harper, Wilkins, the children, and Gracelynn, all settled into the Brinley house quite well. Nan Trea had stayed on as well. She had been such a huge part of the family and the children's lives over the years that they offered her a permanent position in the Brinley home.

Gracelynn spent the whole first week crying on and off over the betrayal and involvement of Derek. She still loved the man. His betrayal hurt terribly, but it didn't eliminate almost forty years of marriage, love, and trust on her part. Neitha would sit and console Gracelynn most days, while Harper and Nan Trea would tend to the children. On other days, Harper sat and cried with her mother.

Wilkins and Harper spent the next month just being with their children and each other. They took little family get a-ways, but not too far, for fear of Raif Martray, Vonder Mortruff, and any number of allies they had in their employment making an appearance. As long as they didn't stray outside the borders of Loradin and the surrounding smaller cities and towns they would be safe. Harper still couldn't help but look over her shoulder whenever they were out in populated areas. She had lived looking over her shoulder for the last three years, and it wasn't a habit she could easily break.

Wilkins tried to encourage her whenever he noticed her get jumpy and fearful, watching everything and everyone around them. He tried hard to get her to relax, and she tried to do so herself, but she never could completely let go. Only when they were in the safety of Aaric and Neitha's home could she let her guard down.

After a month of settling in and things starting to get back to normal, it was time to put the kids back into the academy. They would, however, go to a local academy instead of sending Bain all the way to Port-Proud. He was close to graduating anyway, and his grandfather Aaric had secured all of his papers and was able to place him in a position at the LSS a few months early. He would begin apprenticing with the lab technicians of the LSS.

Young Seadon began the airship academy under the occasional tutelage and guidance of Captain Easton, the man who flew the airship for the LSS. Seadon technically still had a few months of primary academy left, but since he had been placed in FAZ in Port-Proud at the age of eight, the local chapter of FAZ in Loradin allowed him to begin secondary flight academy early.

Young Wynne would attend the primary academy in Loradin for a while longer. She still hadn't found her talent and was a bit worried about it. Harper and Wilkins both assured her that she would find it soon. She just needed to be patient.

Harper stayed at home with little Adda and bonded with her baby girl. Adda still preferred Gracelynn over Harper, but she understood why. Gracelynn did however try to encourage Adda toward Harper as much as she could. Harper needed time with the children, alone, and Gracelynn needed a new life now that taking care of the children was no longer her job.

Gracelynn needed something to look forward to, so she bought an apartment not too far away from the heart of the city. She was only fifteen minutes from Aaric and Neitha's and could visit as often as she liked, and the kids could come spend the night with her if they chose to. She needed to make her own way in life now. She didn't need the money, but she did need something to keep her occupied. Before marriage, her talent had been acting. She was once a well-known and sought-after performer. Because of this, she was able to secure a position as director at the Loradin Theater. A job she was certain she would thoroughly enjoy.

After a few months, Harper and Wilkins began looking for a place of their own. A place where they could resume their lives in some sort of normalcy. Aaric and Neitha assured them they could stay there as long as they wanted, but they wanted and needed their own place. So, Aaric and Neitha offered their home to Wilkins and Harper. It was much too large for them anyway, so they decided to purchase an apartment in the same building as Gracelynn, almost next door to her. It would make it easier for family get-togethers, and for when the grandchildren wanted to visit. Nan Trea would stay on as the children's nanny, living with Wilkins and Harper.

Months went by, and Harper, although she loved being home with little Adda, began to grow restless. She wasn't the same woman as when she was first taken away from her children. She felt almost useless now. She knew in her mind that she wasn't, and that she was doing what she should, but she felt like she needed to do more to protect her family. She could never shake the uneasy feeling of always being watched. She started working at the LSS three days a week to give her something to do. On those days, Nan Trea would take Adda one day, and Neitha and Gracelynn would take the other two days. Everyone got what they wanted and were happy with the situation. The children were all settling in nicely with their new lives and academies, and both sets of grandparents saw them as often as they wanted.

Uncle Finn and Aunt Paisley spoiled the kids rotten. Harper smiled every time she saw Finn playing with one of them. She sometimes saw a sadness in Finn when he held little Adda. Finn had never gone into details about his children, but Harper assumed that he must have had a little girl much like Adda. For it was when he held her that Harper noticed the sadness set in. Finn would hug and squeeze little Adda a little longer than her other three children. Harper's heart ached for her friend each time she witnessed it. She never brought it up to him, figuring if he wanted to talk about it, he would.

One morning Harper woke with a desire to show Wilkins and the kids her treehouse in the Xantifal Mountains. It had been the only other place during her three years of running where she could rest easy. They made a plan for that weekend to take an airship and make a day of it. The entire family went along, including Aaric, Neitha, Gracelynn, Nan Trea, Finn, Paisley, and about ten more LSS agents. They all climbed into the airship for the four-and-a-half-hour flight to the ridge line of the Xantifal Mountains. The airship put down in Storm Valley, and the large party, thoroughly weaponized against the Kabihanxu and Pagorinxes, walked the rest of the way up. Six of the LSS agents stayed behind to guard the airship and its crew against wild animals.

Harper and Finn led the way toward the massive tree. When they got close, Wilkins suddenly stopped.

"What is it, Will?" Harper questioned him.

"When I came through the portal from the other time-period, I saw this tree. It was late fall, and the trees were near barren of leaves. This thing stood out like a beacon. You couldn't miss it. It amazes me to think that you lived here, almost all winter long, alone. Probably not long after I passed through here."

Harper grinned sadly at him, lacing her fingers in his, and they continued to walk, both of them scanning the upper branches for animals.

"Stay close kids. There are some very large, very predatory animals up here," Harper warned.

She showed them the root cellar, the door she had made, the inside of the tree, the bed she had fashioned, and the large split.

They stood in the split, gazing out at Storm Valley and the Xantifal Mountains. It was a sight to behold. Spring was in full bloom and the mountains smelled of fragrant flowers as the wind blew through the colorful canopies of the trees. Leaves in shades of gold, green, blue, and purple floated past, falling over the valley and the ridge line. Wilkins stood behind Harper, wrapping his arms around her as they gazed at the striking landscape around them.

"I would have never thought that you would be able to live like this. To do all the things you've done to survive. I always knew you were an amazing woman, Harper. I just didn't know how amazing you truly are," Wilkins said appreciatively.

"You never know what you're capable of until you have no other choice. I just did what I needed to survive and get back to my family," Harper said, both of them glancing back at their children who played in the expanse of the split.

"You did more than that, Harper. Most people, men included, would have just done what the Scaithers told them to. Not many would have fought the way you did. You could have died taking out that weapon and inciting that rebellion."

"I didn't think about that. I just knew that I couldn't allow them to use it again. I often wonder how many people died that day, Will. How many children, like ours, were killed or orphaned?"

"I know, Harper, but you aren't responsible. You had to build it, or others would have died in the process. You said Martray threatened the other scientists and your mom and the kids if you didn't finish it."

"Yes, and that makes me as guilty of being an accomplice to murder as my father."

"No. That is way different Harper. Your father was involved much deeper than that."

"I know. But it doesn't feel different."

Wilkins could see the pain in her eyes as she spoke. He would give anything if he could take it all away.

"I know how you feel. As an S.O. I had to do a lot of things that I wish I could change. But we can't change the past, all we can do is live for our future. The future we deserve. The one we almost lost out on completely."

She gazed into the eyes of her husband for a few seconds, each understanding the other's pain. They turned to look out the split again hearing the cry of a Kabihanxu far off in the distance. They watched from the safety of the treehouse as the large, four-legged, bird-like creature soared through the bright, blue, sky, high above the mountains, far away on the other side of Storm Valley. It screeched one long, lonely, cry, into the air surrounding the untouched beauty of the Xantifal Mountains.

If you enjoyed reading this book, please leave me a review at whatever venue from which you purchased it. Reviews get my books out there and help to support my writing career. You can also use the "Contact the author page" on my website to leave your review. It will be posted to my website in the reviews section. Thank you, and many blessings to you all.

About the Author

SG Boudreaux is a stay-at-home mom who has home-schooled her children for the last twenty years. Two have graduated, and her youngest is a seventeen-year-old, special-needs child. She and her husband of twenty-five years live in the country, in a small rural area, just outside of Lake Charles, Louisiana. She was born in West Virginia, lived in Florida for many years before moving to Louisiana with her mother and youngest sister. She married a local boy and has lived there ever since. She loves the culture, the people, the sense of community, and definitely the wonderful Cajun food. You can find out more about her and her books on her website at www.sgboudreaux.com

All of her previous books are clean-reading, fiction, fantasy, and time-travel.

You can write to her at the address in the front of the book.

Watch for the second book in the series *Zanchier* to be released late 2021.

Other Books by SG Boudreaux

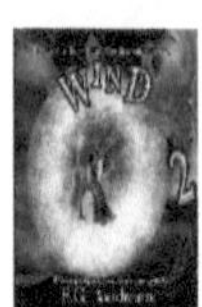

Nonficiton books by Shawna Boudreux

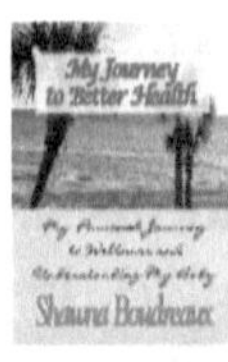
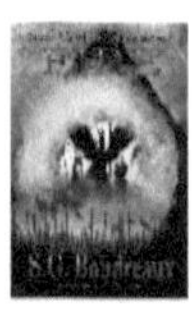

New Releases coming in the Summer of 2023